MONSTERS UNDER MY BED

M.J. MARSTENS

MONSTERS
UNDER MY
BED

TABLET OF CONTENTS

PRONUNCIATION & NOTE	ix
DEDICATION	xi
ONE	1
TWO	8
THREE	15
FOUR	28
FIVE	37
SIX	46
SEVEN	53
EIGHT	59
NINE	65
TEN	72
ELEVEN	81
TWELVE	89
THIRTEEN	97
FOURTEEN	108
FIFTEEN	117
SIXTEEN	125
SEVENTEEN	133
EIGHTEEN	141
NINETEEN	153
TWENTY	162
TWENTY-ONE	170
TWENTY-TWO	179
TWENTY-THREE	190
MONSTERS IN MY BED	197
CRAVING MORE MONSTERS	199
ABOUT M.J. MARSTENS	201
FINAL ACKNOWLEDGEMENTS	203

Copyright © 2021 by M.J. Marstens
All rights reserved.

No part of this publication may be reproduced, stored or transmitted in any form or by any means, electronic, mechanical, photocopying, recording, scanning, or otherwise without written permission from the publisher.

It is illegal to copy this book, post it to a website, or distribute it by any other means without permission.

This novel is entirely a work of fiction. The names, characters and incidents portrayed in it are the work of the author's imagination. Any resemblance to actual persons, living or dead, events or localities is entirely coincidental.

M.J. Marstens asserts the moral right to be identified as the author of this work.

M.J. Marstens has no responsibility for the persistence or accuracy of URLs for external or third-party Internet Websites referred to in this publication and does not guarantee that any content on such Websites is, or will remain, accurate or appropriate."

"Designations used by companies to distinguish their products are often claimed as trademarks. All brand names and product names used in this book and on its cover are trade names, service marks, trademarks and registered trademarks of their respective owners. The publishers and the book are not associated with any productor vendor mentioned in this book. None of the companies referenced within the book have endorsed the book.

First edition

Cover by *Cauldron Press Book Design*

Interior Art by *Lana Brown (Jupiter Moth) and H. Fuzhu*

Edited by *Fine Line Editing*

Formatted by *Inked Imagination Author Services*

PRONUNCIATION GUIDE

Xhoshad (red-eyed monster): *Zo-shawd*

Nerazi (yellow-eyed monster): *Ner-oz-ee*

Seriq (green-eyed monster): *Sair-ick*

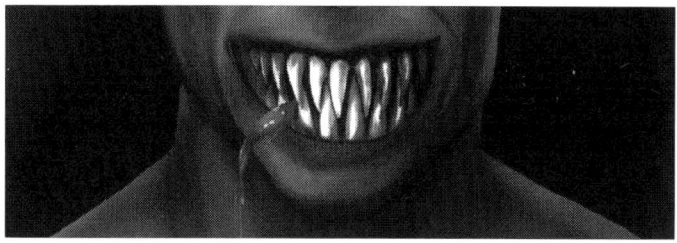

IMPORTANT AUTHOR NOTE

This a reverse harem monster romance. This means the FMC has a relationship with multiple men, including sexually. There are graphic sex scenes, violence, and swearing, often all three together. If you came just for the monster peen, slow your thirsty-ass roll. There's a story to tell, too. You might start to get bangxiety. Don't panic. I repeat: DON'T PANIC.

Fuckery happens. Have your vibe charged or a human cock ready. Maybe you're extra a.f. and own a monster dildo. This can be your companion book when you use it. Don't know what a monster cock looks like? I added a picture in the dedication and in chapter eighteen. On a final note, my FMC has suffered trauma. How she resolves and moves on from this is unique to her, as is everyone's healing process.

BANGXIETY
/ baŋ-ˈzī-ə-tē /
noun

When you are 65% into a romance and the main characters haven't had sex yet and you start to worry that you might be reading a "clean romance".

DEDICATION

FOR ALL THE MONSTER LOVERS.
Enjoy.

ONE

*G**lowing red eyes stare down at me.*

I'm pinned to my bed, my hands and feet tied to the bedpost. Struggle is futile, and my captor's smug smile says he's got me right where he wants me. My chest heaves, thrusting my breasts toward his face—*and what a monstrous face it is*. Scarlet orbs for eyes that blaze in the dark of my room. Up close, I can see the black slits for pupils, like a reptile. A flattened nose above wide, full lips. Inside that mouth, a horror of sparkling, white teeth sharper than a shark and just as dangerous. Behind them hides a foot-long tongue salivating to taste me. Purplish skin completes the nightmare.

"This is just a dream. This is just a dream."

If possible, the creature's smile grows even wider, exposing ivory teeth stained crimson at the base.

Please don't be blood.

I tremble as the man—*if you can call him that*—runs a clawed hand over my face delicately. My breath hitches while I struggle not to move a muscle. In fascination, I watch his taloned fingers dissolve into shadows, gliding over my skin like a ghost. Despite my rapt attention, I blink, hoping to dispel the scene before me. Just like that, the monster disappears—only for another to emerge seconds later. His features are similar, except for the eyes. They're a bright, nearly-blinding yellow and his skin has more pink tinted throughout the dark violet.

"J-j-just a dream," I repeat on a stammer, making the new monster laugh in delight.

He doesn't bother responding, but his amusement vibrates through my exposed body. I'm wearing a soft pink babydoll that reveals more than it covers, making me shiver in vulnerability. I strain against the ropes holding me back, the rough material chafing the delicate flesh at my wrists. Something wet traces along the inside of my thigh as I attempt to squirm out of reach. Another rumble of laughter assaults my ears, and I feel a hot puff of air against my aching, traitorous core. Moment by agonizing moment, I wait for the beast to continue, squeezing my eyes tightly shut.

But my legs fall open of their own accord, the muscles shaking in fear and anticipation.

When nothing happens, I tentatively slit open one eye, peeking beneath my lashes. The sight that greets me steals the oxygen right from my lungs, as if someone snaked a hand inside my chest to take it. The yellow-eyed monster is gone; in his wake is another with vivid chartreuse eyes. He stands at the foot of the bed, a combination of tangibility and smoke—half-shadow, half-man.

In the dim light cast from his eyes, I can see his torso and arms roped by thick, smooth muscles. He's naked, but my position and the bed stops me from seeing anything below where a belly button should be. Against my better intentions, I stretch forward to see more. I'm rewarded by the ropes snapping me back into place, but not before I saw a silhouetted hand stroking a massive—

A growl from the monster captures my attention.

He doesn't say anything—he never does—but his gaze never leaves mine. Neon flames burn in those depths, promising me pain and pleasure in equal measure. Where I once angled my body to break free, I now turn toward the man in supplication. Only he can quell the fire threatening to scorch me alive, but like the nightmare this is, the green-eyed monster does no such thing. In fact, he steps back further into the darkness of my room. Two other pairs of glowing eyes join his from the black of the night.

"Please!" I beg on a gasp, not sure what I really want—for them to leave...

Or to stay.

Either way, it doesn't matter because, one by one, they slowly fade away. I scream into the night in fright and vexation, but only taunting laughter greets me.

"Sssssoon," a voice sibilates, and I tremble.

Soon what?

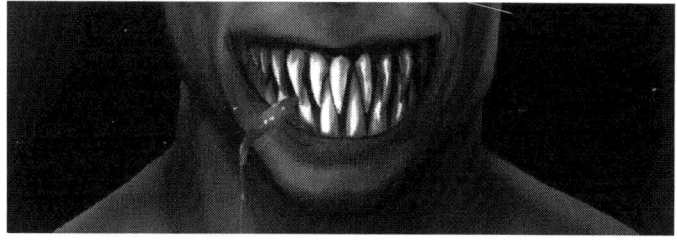

I wake up terrified.

Disturbed.

Wet.

My heart racing, I lay there panting, trying to calm my breathing. I try to sort through the jumbled state of my emotions. A light scratching that haunts my dreams sounds from under my bed and I freeze, my blood running cold.

Maybe it hadn't been a dream after all.

I inhale sharply, holding my trembling breath inside my lungs, refusing to exhale.

Scratch, scratch.

My chest burns with the need for oxygen.

Scratch, scratch.

Finally, I can't take it anymore. A rush of air escapes my lips, whistling into the dark of my bedroom. I squint my eyes, trying to discern my surroundings. Finally, I reach over for my phone, but it's missing. Baffled, I stiffly try to turn on my lamp without creating a ruckus, but there's nothing on my nightstand. My heart hammers painfully in my breast while I will my brain to work. Pushing past the lingering images of my dream, I recall that I'm not in my childhood bedroom—and no monsters live here.

Or do they?

The thought squeezes my throat like a vice, as if one of the monster's shadowed hands has reached out to wrap around it. I claw at my neck, but it's only my panic suffocating me. Nearly convulsing violently, I remember I don't have a lamp in this room. Instead, I installed clap-on lights exactly for times *like this*. Pulling my hands together sharply—relieved they aren't actually tied to my bedpost—I applaud my brilliant idea as soft light filters throughout my room. Relief slams through me.

Until I hear the scratching again.

Irritation wars with my fear. The monsters don't like the light—*why are they still lingering?* I nibble on my lip, gathering my courage to investigate like I did all those years ago. Tentatively, I peer over the edge of my bed. Like that fateful night, I don't see anything—but I still hear the scratching sound. *Strange.* Reminding myself that I'm a grown woman with nothing to fear, I push off my comforter. Leaping nimbly off my bed, I launch my body swiftly across the room where I turn on my overhead light.

The clappers aren't good enough right now.

With excruciating slowness, I lower onto my knees, creeping at a snail's pace on all fours back toward my bed. To cover my nerves, I mentally berate myself for not buying a bed that sat on the ground. *Nothing can hide under your bed if there's no space, right?* Unfortunately, my apartment already came with a frame, and I don't have enough space to store it. Those first few weeks were harrowing, but it seemed I'd finally escaped my monsters. In twelve years, they'd never found me.

Until tonight.

As I edge closer, I lower my front to the wooden floor, pressing myself flush to the ground. My pulse jumps like a rabbit's, the rhythmic throbbing reminding me of the fluttering torment I felt between my legs when I woke up. Steeling my spine at the absurdity of my current position, I force myself to look under the bed. A sensation similar to being high courses my veins when I find nothing there. *It was just a dream.* Except, I hear that damned familiar scratching sound again. Pissed with the mindfuck, I push off the ground and shove at my bed. Something immediately clatters to the ground, making me jump like a frightened mouse.

It's my phone.

I must have fallen asleep and dropped it behind my iron-wrought headboard, where it became jammed between the bed and the wall. A second item drops down as my phone vibrates, making the familiar scraping noise. Upon closer look, it's just a candy wrapper—I eat foil-encased chocolate in bed to soothe my pre-bed jitters... at least, that's what I tell my therapist. The vibration of my phone against the candy wrapper made an eerily similar sound to the one that skulked unsolicited in my memories. Sighing at the ridiculous scenario I currently am in, I stretch my arm to retrieve both my phone and the small square of foil. Licking a speck of melted chocolate that escaped my tongue previously, I ponder my dream.

Moreover, my body's reaction.

It wasn't uncommon to have nightmares—my demons from fifteen years ago were always in the back of my mind—but they usually didn't devolve into me begging for release. Turning my phone over, the illuminated screen reads three twenty-seven in the morning, and I have multiple text messages. *They're from my dad.* I opened them, hoping nothing is wrong. My mom died eleven years ago, and I'm all he has left. I begged him to move to Australia, but he won't budge. The man is a Texan, through and through. According to him, everything isn't only bigger, but better, in Texas.

When I click into the message, it's not from my dad but a nurse from Harris Hospital. The obstinate man had a heart attack and wasn't cooperating well with hospital staff—no surprise there. There were complications after his emergency surgery, and he needed care. Although this nurse doesn't know me, she took it upon herself to text me because dad never would have. Hell, if not for this unknown woman, I might never have learned about his hospital stint!

Heaven forbid a Texan man be weak.

Swallowing thickly, I stare at my phone, my hands shaking slightly. *Go home?* I hadn't been to the States in over twelve years—*not since I'd fled them.* There was a reason I moved half-way across the world, but it would seem that my time is up. Dad needs me. I'd run for long enough. I shoot the nurse a text saying I would get there as soon as humanly possible. Travel from Australia to the U.S. wasn't quick, even by plane. Her reply is short and simple.

Hurry. His condition isn't stable.

I blink at the sentence, going back to the original message sent only hours before. *How had he deteriorated so fast?* With a heavy heart, I pull out a suitcase and begin to pack while simultaneously booking a flight back home. Although I'm worried sick about my dad, I welcome the distraction.

Anything to erase the memory of monsters between my legs.

TWO

Texas in August is like Hell at high noon.

This time of year is actually winter in Australia. While it's still warm, it's *nothing* like the sauna I've just stepped into. I blink as the bright sunlight burns my eyelids as I disembark. Over my shoulder rests the strap of a single carry-on bag—a testimony of my rush to get here *and* my promise not to linger any longer than I need to.

Help my dad recover and then get back to Oz.

The taxi drive from the airport to my rural hometown has me on pins and needles. When I tell the cabbie where I'm heading, he wastes no time getting me there. Too soon, we arrive, my nerves creating a jumbled ball of jittery tension in my stomach. Screw butterflies—it feels like a bomb is about to detonate inside my gut, splattering my intestines all over the side of Harris Hospital. The vivid picture makes me grimace, but distracts me a bit as I try to envision workers scraping off the bloody debris.

I would not want that job.

A smile tugs at my lips at my irrational musings, and I make a note to tell Dr. Lola, my therapist. We've been working on using mental imagery to redirect my thoughts from points of fear to ones of empowerment. I doubt thinking of my midsection blowing up and painting a building in shades of macabre is what she had in mind, though. I'm terrified to walk into the hospital and face a man I haven't seen in twelve years—to see how he's deteriorated. The burden of my guilt already weighs my shoulders down. *I don't need any more added to it.* A man at the reception desk directs me to the second floor when I inquire about my father. Steadily, I make my way there, stopping at the nurses' station once I'm there.

"Hi, I'm Alexis Stanton—" I start to the woman, but she cuts me off.

"Alexis! So nice to meet you. I'm who you spoke with via text."

I nod and tentatively put out my hand to shake.

"It's nice to meet you, too. Thank you for reaching out to me."

The nurse waves a dismissive hand.

"It was nothing. Your father didn't want us to bother you, but he doesn't have anyone else to care for him, and he wants out of this hospital."

I sigh at her words.

"Sounds like my dad. How's he doing?"

"Currently, he's resting and recovering. He's stable and likely to be released soon, but he definitely needs somebody at home with him. We're concerned because he's refusing all care."

Now, I roll my eyes.

"Definitely sounds like him."

"Your father's in room 207, if you want to go see him. It's just about time for dinner—maybe you can get him to eat something."

"He's not eating?" I whisper, my worry ratcheting up a notch, but the woman in front of me waves her hand again.

"Only because the man's picky. Story of my life! He doesn't want to eat *hospital* food—then again, no one does, but if he wants to be released, he has to eat something."

My shoulders release at her words, and the tension ebbs out of me.

"You would think he would've done it already to get out of here, but I'll see what I can do."

I don't have high expectations, but don't tell the friendly nurse this. I haven't seen the man in over twelve years and haven't spoken to him since last Christmas. Things aren't the best between us, not since my mother passed when I was nineteen, and I refused to come home. I know how shitty that sounds, but nobody understands the situation I was in—*I couldn't go back home.* Hell, I shouldn't be here now but I'm a grown woman—almost thirty—it's time for me to face my fears. What scared me as an impressionable teen shouldn't still scare me. Of course, this is all bravado.

I'm petrified to be back home.

But I realized when I got those text messages that I really couldn't live with myself if I didn't return. The door to my dad's room is closed, and I knock briefly before peeking in. I drink in the sight of the man I haven't laid eyes on in over a decade. He refuses to keep up with technology and barely can operate his phone to call me, let alone video chat. His light brown hair is mostly white, peppered with some streaks of the color I remember from my youth. He's still a big guy, but lying on the bed, tubes hooked into both his arms, makes him seem feebler.

More fragile.

His eyes are half-mast, staring at a TV screen, like he's ready to doze off. The sound of my entry briefly alerts him, and dad looks over uninterested, as if expecting a nurse. When his gaze locks with mine, his blue eyes, so like my own, widen in shock, mingled with profound relief and happiness.

"Lexi Bug?! Is that really you?" he croaks.

Tears fill my eyes at the nickname I didn't know how much I missed until this moment.

"Yeah, dad, it's me. I've come home to take care of you."

I shuffle awkwardly into the room and lean over to give him a hug, careful not to pull on any of the numerous IV lines. "How are you doing?"

It's a lame question considering we haven't seen one another in years, and he's recuperating from a heart attack.

"Ok, but between this and the fall—"

"What fall?" I interject sharply, and my dad blanches.

"I forgot to tell you, kiddo. It happened last winter after the holidays." Now, I flinch because I never reached out to him after Christmas. Blinking back ashamed tears, my brain tries to catch up on what he's saying. "...you know that old house—it's been harder to keep up in recent years."

I nod, somewhat understanding. My childhood home is a classic farmhouse that's been passed down for generations on my dad's side of the family. It's definitely seen better days —*twelve years ago*. I can only imagine how it is now.

"I'll admit I've kind of let it go..." Dad continues, shifting uncomfortably before confessing, "I guess I've kind of let myself go, too. With you and your mom gone... I just haven't had much to live for."

His words reach out and grip me around my throat, strangling me until I choke on their bitter truth. My guilt from earlier comes roaring back to the surface, weighing me down even more as if gravity has been intensified.

"Dad," I attempt, but my voice cracks. "I'm... *so* sorry. I've been busy with work and should've call—"

He cuts off my excuses.

"Lexi, it's time to let bygones be bygones. Was I mad you didn't come back home for your mom? Yes. Her dying wish was that she wanted to see you." I wince, biting the inside of my cheek so hard I taste the metallic tang of blood. "But I can't change the past—*and neither can you*. All that matters to me now is that you're here."

He reaches up to give me another hug, and I lean down to meet him half-way, moved by his words and total absolution of all my transgressions. At least one of us has forgiven me.

"I missed you, daddy."

"I missed you, too, Lexi Bug. Now, I know you're a big shot photographer at some firm, but tell me more about your life in Australia. You got any boyfriends? Are there any grandkids in my future?" he wonders too eagerly, making me laugh.

"Sorry, dad. No to both."

"Well, you don't need to be married nowadays to have kids," my dad points out.

"Someone's eager to be a grandpa, but it's all out of the picture for the time being. Maybe in a few years," I hedge.

"I suppose, but you're not getting any younger—and neither am I!" I frown at the reminder of his inevitable mortality, but dad snaps his fingers, "Say—what about your old flame from high school? He's still single! Why don't I see—"

I hastily stand up, raising both hands, putting an abrupt stop to his match-making.

"That's ok, Dad, thank you, but I'm just here for *you*. Speaking of you, the nurse said you're not eating anything?"

My question effectively turns my dad's attention. He frowns and harrumphs, folding his arms loosely over his chest.

"The food here is nasty!" he scowls.

"I'm sure it is," I soothe, "but they're not going to let you out of here if you don't eat anything."

His glare intensifies before crumbling in surrender.

"I guess you're right," he grumbles, tugging a small smile from my lips at his petulant attitude.

"How about I make you a deal? *If* you eat some of the hospital food, I will sneak you in some Grumpy's. I bet by tomorrow afternoon we can get you home."

Dad grins at this plan, a wistful look of yearning in his eyes.

"I miss home. You always were the best, Lexi Bug. Thank you."

"No problem, dad. I'll go get you something now to snack on."

"Just get me the *least* nastiest thing you can find—if that's possible. But I want a cheeseburger and onion rings in return!"

"Deal! Let me go talk to the nurse. I'll notify her that you're going to eat and see if I can stay in the waiting room."

"No, no, no! I want you to go home—you can sleep there tonight."

I clutch my hands together to hide the violent trembling coursing through them as I shake my head adamantly in refusal.

"That's ok, Dad, I need to stay here in case anything happens to you."

"Nothing's gonna happen to me, kiddo—I'm *in* a hospital. Besides, Mr. Mittens needs you."

I latch onto his words like a life raft—anything to keep me from sinking into my own thoughts and fears.

"Mr. Mittens?! That cat has to be a hundred and eighty! How is he still alive?" I attempt to joke.

"I imagine he's clinging on for me, poor thing, but he's a good companion. I don't want Mrs. Williams to have to keep taking care of him. Could you please go home and tend to the house?"

I hesitate briefly before agreeing.

"Sure, Dad," I promise, knowing it's an absolute lie.

I don't want to go back to that house, and certainly not by myself. I know I came back to conquer my fears…

But I have no intention of meeting them face-to-face.

CHAPTER

THREE

I'm so busy making plans to put two chairs together as a make-shift bed in the waiting room —my dad's wish be damned—that I'm not paying any attention to my surroundings. As I round a hall corner toward the hospital cafeteria, I bump into an all-too familiar face. *One I haven't seen in over twelve years.* It's not just my family I ran out on, but this entire town, including the man I just plowed into, Mark Bradley.

"Mark!" I squeak in surprise.

"Alexis," he breathes in the same shocked tone. His face lights up with a disbelieving, sweet smile that still makes my heart melt. "You came back."

These three simple words freeze my liquefied insides into ice that shatters painfully in my breast.

"Only for a little bit to help my dad," I quickly clarify, not wanting Mark to get any ideas of why I came back or that I might be staying.

I know everybody in Cleburne thinks I'm a selfish nutcase that ditched her family and boyfriend; then when I didn't come back for my own mom's funeral, it just sealed the deal.

Alexis Stanton was—is—a monster.

"I should explain..." I start hesitantly, but Mark lifts a hand.

"You *don't* owe me any explanations or any apology. I'm just glad to see you again and move on from here," he echoes words similar to my dad's, adding to my growing compunction.

Honestly, if the guilt gets any more suffocating, this man is going to have to give me CPR—not that this would be a terrible thing. Mark Bradley was a specimen years ago when we were just teens. *Now, he's a glorified God.* His wavy, brown hair is trimmed at the sides, but longer on top, flopping down across his forehead artfully. His golden eyes are framed by dark lashes perfectly off-set by his patrician nose and full lips. To top it all off, the man has dimples and the biggest, whitest smile I've ever seen. He's wearing a fitted suit that does *nothing* to hide his physique underneath. A tag on his jacket catches my eye.

"Dr. Bradley, huh? You always said you were going to be a doctor."

"And *you* always said you were going to be my nurse," he teases.

I laugh because that's not exactly what I said—I told him I was going to be his *naughty nurse*. When you're eighteen, you say some pretty dumb shit.

"I remember those days," I smile at Mark.

"And those nights," he adds, his honey-brown eyes turning molten.

I swallow thickly at the reminder that he was my first, but on the heels of that thought is the remembrance of *them*. It seemed the more active Mark and I got, the more the shadows under my bed came out to play. I slam a door on those thoughts, quickly locking them back where they belong, and paste a bright, fake smile on my lips. Scrambling to change the subject, I glance down at the papers in his hand. My brows scrunch at the metaphysical jargon talking about black hole portals.

"Are you also a doctor of astronomy?" I tease, indicating to what he's holding.

"Hmmm? Oh, no, just an.... interest. There are so many unexplained phenomena; if only we knew...." he smiles, trailing off and tucking the papers behind his back. "Sorry, I get lost in trying to find answers. This is actually more about physics than astronomy, although I dabble in both."

"I thought your hobby was writing," I return, wondering what answers Mark is searching for.

He shrugs.

"People change—especially when you haven't spoken to them in over a decade."

He doesn't say this cruelly, but I feel the sting of his words all the same.

"True. Er, it was really good to see you, Mark, but I have to go get my dad some food," I excuse myself politely.

Mark, being the sweetheart he is, doesn't miss a beat.

"Of course, I completely understand. Apologies if my words made you uncomfortable." I dip my head in acknowledgement, although his words didn't bother me like he thinks. "I'm surprised your dad's eating," Mark continues, tripping a genuine laugh from lips.

"Only because I had to bribe him! I told him I would get Grumpy's if he ate a little bit of the food here."

Mark raises a brow.

"Has his doctor cleared this?" he demands more seriously, making me shift uncomfortably.

"Um, I don't know who his doctor... I mean, no, not tech—"

Mark cuts me off by tipping his head back and laughing uproariously at my chagrin. The sound is mesmerizing, but not nearly as mesmerizing as he is to look at. It wakes up feelings long dormant inside of me for him—things I thought I only felt for monsters.

Maybe there is some hope for me to be normal yet.

"*I'm* his doctor, Lexie," Mark chuckles, and his use of my old nickname makes me shiver, reminding me of the more intimate times when he used it.

"How awfully convenient you're his doctor," I murmur, wondering if my dad has talked to the man about his lack of grandchildren. "Well, Dr. Bradley, I'm bribing my dad with Grumpy's. I hope that's ok."

"I'll let it slide, but only because he's on the mend," the sexy man smirks.

My thighs subconsciously squeeze together at Mark's expression, both playful and flirtatious.

"Do you think you can get him out of this joint early then?" I tease, leaning slightly into my old boyfriend's personal space before pulling away, realizing that I'm flirting right back.

I frown, wondering what has gotten into me, but Mark is like the sun, sucking me into his orbit. With every passing second, I relax into his company, getting more and more comfortable. If I'm not careful, I'm going to lose my head, as well as my heart.

"Your dad will probably be released tomorrow afternoon, pending that all his blood work comes back fine."

"That's great. He really wants to go home." I breathe, straightening until my spine feels like it's going to snap. I shove at my heavy dark blonde hair clinging to my nape.

The Texas humidity hasn't permeated the hospital hall, but I'm sweating like a sinner in Sunday church. The rollercoaster of emotions I've felt in the last twenty-four hours is enough to last me a lifetime. The last thing I need added to that dizzying cocktail is *attraction*. Thankfully, Mark has taken on a more professional tone, talking about my dad. I promised myself that I came back here to face my fears—*not have a fling*.

"I know your dad wants out of here. Home is definitely where his heart is. I think he's been waiting a long time to finally get his daughter back there with him. I know I've been. Twelve years is a long time without even a phone call."

Mark's words make the muscles in my body tense involuntarily. The familiar stress of returning and facing everyone I left behind comes rushing back to the forefront of my mind. I suppose I should thank Mark. His words remind me why I need to keep to myself. My dad might say that he doesn't want an explanation or an apology, but he does want something—for me to stay.

"Well, I better get going. Thank you so much for taking care of my dad."

Mark stuffs his hands into his pockets while rocking back on his heels and biting the inside of his left cheek. It hollows out his sculpted face even more, highlighting where his dimple is.

"You don't have to thank me for doing my job. I'm just glad that he's doing better, but he's getting older, Lexie. His health isn't the best, and…"

He trails off, but I already know his unspoken warning. My dad only has so much longer on this earth, and I shouldn't waste it living half a world away. What Mark doesn't understand is that Australia is safe. There, my monsters only torment me in my nightmares. I would ask dad to move there with me in a heartbeat, but I know his heart is in that old farmhouse. Trying to make this less awkward, I slowly start edging down the hall, away from Mark. Being a gentleman, he lets me skate away, but when I'm about to turn another corner and blissfully escape his line of sight, Mark yells out to me.

"Alexis!"

My feet inadvertently freeze, halting me in my tracks.

"Yeah?" I call back, hunching my shoulders together in a protective manner against the words I fully expect and deserve to hear, but they never come.

Instead, what Mark shouts out is even worse than the doctorly rebuke of not sticking around to help take care of my dad.

"I waited—when you left, I waited every day for you to come back."

His words make me wonder if someone can physically die of guilt. I swear I can feel it eating a hole through my gut. I don't respond because I have no rebuttal to the man who waited for me so selflessly. Instead, I just nod, letting him know I heard his words.

How could I not?

They've pierced my heart.

I turn away, scurrying toward the cafeteria, but not before Mark's final words float over to me.

"And I'll wait a hundred years more, Lexie. I'll always wait for you. You're the girl I'm not letting go."

Hot tears sting my eyes at his poignant vow. I don't deserve his kindness, nor his forgiveness, and especially not his love.

Doesn't he get I'm the very thing I fear—nothing more than a heartless monster.

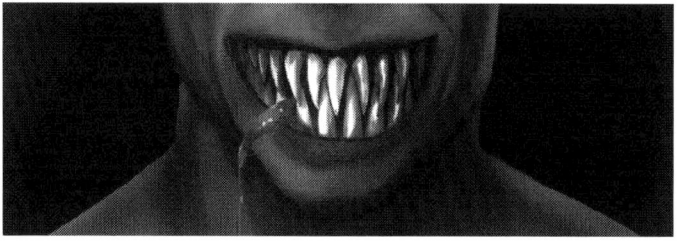

"Damnit, Dad, you promised!" I burst out in frustration, almost relieved to have something constructive to funnel my overload of emotions into, but the man doesn't look the least bit repentant at having broken his word.

"I lied. It's ok because I'm old and sick," he retorts, and I roll my eyes at his antics.

Like a dutiful daughter—more like a daughter trying to make up for her years of absence and neglect—I bought my dad Grumpy's after I left him to eat some hospital jello. It was the least innocuous thing I could grab, even if it was a radioactive yellow. The neon color is one of my least favorites, right after green and red.

They bring to mind three pairs of captivating, inhuman eyes.

I blink rapidly to dispel the effulgent glow that seems permanently burned into my retinas. Dad is horking down his cheeseburger like he hasn't eaten in days. *For all I know, he hasn't.* I'm pretty sure Mark was being lenient when he found out that I was getting this for my dad because, in his health, he shouldn't be eating something that oozes cholesterol and another impending heart attack. I experience more guilt for not encouraging Dad to eat better—to take better care of himself—but mentally argue you only live once, too. I hate to admit it, but he's right about the food here—*it's crap*. I took a chance on some coleslaw and have some serious gastronomical regrets. Unfortunately for Dad, though, his hiding skills are just as much crap as the food in this joint because I find the uneaten jello stashed in the cabinet where I hung my purse.

"You didn't even *try* to dispose of it?" I huff in exasperation.

"No, the nurses check," he deadpans.

"You could've flushed it," I suggest, wondering why I'm giving him ideas.

Dad shifts uncomfortably on the bed.

"They got me hooked up to a colostomy bag. I kept falling..." he trails off in embarrassment, although I'm unsure if it's because of the former or the latter.

I rub my chest where the familiar pang of regret is brewing.

If I had stayed home, would Dad be in the hospital today?

As much as I try not to play 'what if', sometimes the haunting questions sneak up on me and have a party inside my head. They invite all their friends, like disgrace and shame, who toss vicious jibes at my already battered and down-trodden self-esteem.

"Well, at least you won't be clogging any of the toilets with jello," I joke, wrangling a smile from my dad.

"I would hope not—I'm too old and sick for such pranks."

"Says the man who just hid it childishly in the coat cabinet! And you're not *that* old and just a little sick."

"I'm sixty-eight, Lexi Bug, and this is heart attack number two."

I come up short.

"*Number two?* When did you have the other one?"

Dad shrugs like it's no big deal.

"Eh, four or five years ago, I think. I can't really recall the specific year anymore."

"Dad, why didn't you say anything?!" I ask, horrified.

His eyes lock with mine, deep and penetrating.

"I was in and out of the hospital—nothing like this. Besides, would it have changed anything?" he challenges.

I flinch and look away, shamefaced, knowing that he has a point.

"I'm here now," I point out softly.

Dad frowns.

"You're right. You are. S'pose it's just as much my fault as yours. You didn't come home for your mom's funeral, so I didn't think you would come back for something as small as a heart attack."

He's trying to offer me solace, but all he does is add to my burden.

I'm the world's worst daughter.

Dad reaches out with his hand, beckoning me over, and I walk to him. He takes my palm in his and squeezes it gently, an unfathomable look in his eyes.

"Listen, don't be too hard on yourself, kiddo. We all know the incident…" He pauses when I shudder violently at the mention of it. "It was difficult for you. I get that."

I nod, his words the understatement of the century. It wasn't difficult—*it was debilitating*. I barely managed to hack it at life after what happened, and it's taken me *years* to become a semi-normally functioning person. *And that's only on the good days.* Let's just say that the thousands I spend on therapy haven't really fixed very much. Probably because my therapists are attempting some form of closure for me, but I'm still looking for answers.

"Hey, good news," I say brightly, turning the subject, "I bumped into Mark."

"Oh yeah? Your old flame is my doctor," Dad announces, waggling his eyebrows.

"Something you forgot to mention earlier," I chide

sternly. "Please tell me you haven't asked him about us getting married and having grandbabies."

My dad gets a goofy grin on his face.

"I might have mentioned it when he came in a bit ago while you were gone," he concedes.

"Dad!" I burst out, amazed that at thirty years old, he can still embarrass me.

"I'm kidding; I'm kidding! So, what did he have to say?" Dad wonders eagerly—too eagerly.

"Nothing about me—us, er, him and me. We talked about *you*," I huff. "I asked him if maybe you could get out of here tomorrow and go home. Mark said as long as your bloodwork comes back good, then yes!"

A delighted smile lights up my dad's face.

"That's almost as good as you telling me you two talked about giving me grandkids," he winks, making me groan. "I appreciate you asking him. I miss home—I miss your mom."

He adds this last part in a rush before I can yell at him for teasing me again, and I give my dad a sad look.

"Mom's dead, Dad," I remind quietly.

"I know!" he chuckles, surprising me. "But her spirit's at that house."

"What?!" I shriek, like her ghost just popped up. "She haunts the house?!"

Dad's eyes widen at my outburst.

"I didn't mean for real, Alexis! Calm down. I just meant her pictures are there along with her essence."

I nod weakly, feeling relieved.

In my defense, if monsters terrorized my childhood home, why couldn't my mom be a poltergeist?

"Well, you should probably start heading to the house. Mr. Mittens will be waiting. If you don't feed him on time, he gets hangry—and nobody wants a hangry cat. It's the closest thing to demon spawn." Another shiver wracks my body. I doubt a starving Mr. Mittens can hold a candle to the ravenous demon spawn from under my bed. "I texted Mrs. Williams and told her she didn't have to take care of the poor guy tonight because you were coming to keep him company. I can't imagine how lonely he is."

Grimacing, I wonder how I'm going to get to the house and make my dad think I stayed there before sneaking back to the hospital. I highly doubt Mr. Mittens gives two craps whether I stay or not as long as I feed him before I split. All I know is I can't risk staying alone at that house during the night.

Monsters come out to play when the sun sets there.

"Alexis Josephine, I know what you're thinking! Don't come sneaking back here tonight, ya hear me, young lady?" I stifle a smile at my dad's fatherly command, as well as his ability to still read me perfectly after being gone for over a decade. "I promise I'm going to be ok."

I swallow and nod, wondering how shallow I'm being because I'm not one-hundred percent worried about him—there's a good amount of fear for myself.

"I know that you live in the big city," Dad continues, oblivious to my internal struggle, "and being alone in the country is...unnerving. So, I asked Mark to escort you home."

My jaw unhinges and drops open at this announcement.

"Dad—the city is *way* more dangerous than living out here!" I splutter in astonishment.

"Oh, well, I thought you might be ah, uncomfortable, at the house—because of what happened," he rushed to continue, and I close my eyes in an attempt to stop his words. "It was terrible, Lex, but there's nothing wrong with that house. Lived there nigh my whole life and never encountered anything out of the ordinary."

I don't even bother interrupting and trying to explain—I tried eons ago, all it got me was the pretty label of 'mentally unstable'.

"Did you hear me, Lexie Bug?"

"Sorry, I didn't," I mutter, not bothering to point out I was *trying* not to listen.

"I asked Mark to stay with you at the house," he repeats, and I swear my eyes bug out of my head.

"That's... inappropriate," I finish lamely, latching onto the only acceptable excuse not to have Mark spend the night alone with me.

Of course, Dad just rolls his eyes.

"Alexis, it's 2021. Like I said, you don't need to be married to make me grandbabies."

"I'm not "making you" any grandchildren with Dr. Bradley," I retort primly.

"Well, a man can hope. It would probably help speed up my recovery—you know, give me something to look forward to."

"*Now* you start playing the guilt card?" I laugh, but the sound is tinny and off because he has *every* right to wield it against me.

And after everything, how can I possibly say no?

Just like spending the night at the house, I'm going to have to find a way around Mark staying with me.

"Just let him escort you home," Dad insists, again reading my mind, or maybe my facial expressions. Mom always said I was an open book, which sucked when I was a teen and just wanted to keep everything bottled inside. "Mark's missed you as much as I have."

And there was the pièce de résistance of his guilt trip,

executed to perfection. I felt the noose tightening around my neck, inescapable and deadly, because surely staying at that house—*alone or otherwise*—will solidify my doom.

I escaped them once; they won't give me another chance to do it again.

CHAPTER

FOUR

I linger until the night nurse gives Dad his medication and he dozes off to sleep. Silently, I grab my purse and slip out of the room. If I can sneak downstairs and grab a cab, I might be able to evade—

"Wanna catch a bite to eat?"

"Ahhhh!" I yelp, startled.

Whirling around, I come face-to-chest with Mark.

So much for being elusive.

I poke my head back into my dad's room to see if I woke him, but he appears to be sleeping soundly.

"Don't worry, he's been given something to help him rest," Mark whispers in my ear, invoking a whole-body response from my traitorous frame.

My brain frowns censoriously—the only part of me not one hundred percent on board with jumping Mark's bones.

"You scared me!" I burst out in a hushed voice.

"I'm sorry. I didn't mean to," he apologizes. "I've been off work for some time and was just waiting for you."

My shoulders sag at his words.

"You didn't have to wait for me! I'm sure you're tired and want to go home."

"Actually, I'm famished. I didn't stop for lunch today—I was distracted by the most amazing thing."

Mark looks at me expectantly, and it takes a moment for his words to click.

I'm the most amazing thing.

Great, now *he's* adding to my guilt. Again, not that I deserve any less, but my heart and soul need a break. Coming here was a mistake—I just hope I can survive this trip in one piece.

"Come get dinner with me, please?" the gorgeous man in front of me begs.

The night nurse is peeking around her station, shamelessly eavesdropping. The look on her face reminds me of the girls who chase Gaston from *Beauty and the Beast*. It's like I can hear her saying:

What's wrong with her?

He's dreamy.

"I promise to be the perfect gentleman," Mark adds, making me laugh.

"That's *not* something I'm worried about," I chuckle.

Mark has always been one of the most considerate people I've met. Our first time together was due to *my* initiation, not his.

He frowns at my words.

"Do you not want me to be a gentleman?"

The temperature in the hall spikes up a thousand degrees at his question, reminding me of my dream where I was bound and spread for monsters—everything but gagged at that point.

Clearly, I'm not into gentlemen.

Nor gentle monsters.

I want it rough, forceful, and domineering.

"So, ah, dinner?" I ask like a coward. "Not a date, though."

"Not a date," he agrees, "just catch up between old friends."

"Ok, that sounds nice."

I can use some friends around here.

"And maybe a goodnight kiss?" Mark adds playfully, with a hint of buried yearning.

My pulse accelerates at his words, and I have to clear my throat twice before I can answer. The night nurse looks ready to shove me aside to take my place. I give her a pointed look until she thankfully turns back to her desk.

"Do friends *really* kiss goodnight?" I wonder, but a husky note has crept into my voice.

I know Mark hears it because his eyes slip to my mouth. He licks his lips as if anticipating kissing mine later. But it's not his tongue I see, but one about a foot longer, licking along my jawbone. Fidgeting imperceptibly, raw need sizzles a fiery path through my body at the errant thought. Mentally scolding myself, I focus on the man before me, and I'm catapulted back to our first time together. We were both a couple of inept teenagers, but Mark managed to stoke a fire in me back then—rather, my imagination of monstrous beings did.

But that was twelve years ago—*I don't lust for monsters*—maybe I should let Mark show me what he's capable of *now*.

Mark shoves his hands in his pant pockets.

"Some friends kiss," he teases. "But *only* after they've eaten dinner together."

I nibble on my lip before deciding.

"Dinner and a kiss, huh?" I ask, earning me a delighted, if not heated, look from my old boyfriend. "Lead the way."

Mark takes my hands and offers the disappointed night nurse a wave as he escorts me outside. I shiver as we walk out into the hot evening sun.

"Are you cold?" Mark asks.

"No, it's just the transition of going from the air conditioning out into the warmth," I lie, not wanting to confess that my mind is trying to remind me of all the naughty, messed-up things a foot-long tongue could do.

Jesus, why can't I get *them* out of my head? I can go most days without thinking about the monsters that lived under my bed. Heck, I've gone months successfully living my life without them haunting me, but clearly, being back here means they'll be the number one thing on my mind. We get into Mark's Mustang, and he drives me across town to a diner that wasn't there when I left. Cleburne is a small town with few amenities—at least there was when I was growing up.

A grocery store, a family-owned "movie theater", a handful of diners, and a bed and breakfast—not much to write home about, but enough. If you wanted anything bigger, you had to go two cities over to Fort Worth, which was about forty minutes away. Growing up, my parents were generally content to stick around town. My dad ran his own business, and my mom was a secretary-slash-accountant. They were busy a lot when I was a kid. Being an only child, I was often left to my own devices to entertain myself. Luckily, I had plenty of friends to keep occupied during the day.

And a few to keep me up at night.

I cluck my tongue at myself, tuning back to the diner Mark's stopped at. I fully expected him to take us out of town; in fact, I was secretly hoping he would. The further away we got from here, the quicker I could outrun my demons that I supposedly planned to face and conquer.

Do we lie to anyone more than ourselves?

The sign on the diner reads 'Owl's Nest' and, apparently, they have the best waffles and chicken. I wrinkle my nose at the chicken dancing holding a bottle of syrup.

"That sounds… gross," I blurt out undiplomatically, but Mark just laughs.

"Don't knock it until you've tried it! It's really popular in the States now."

"It's *not* in Australia—I mean, at least not where I live."

"Well, you don't have to order that—maybe just some waffles to sweeten your disposition."

I fake gasp in affront.

"Are you saying that I'm not sweet?!"

"Lexie, you're sweeter than sugar, I'm just looking for anything that might butter you up into giving me that goodnight kiss."

"The guilt trip really worked for my dad, if you want to give that angle a shot," I joke.

Mark squeezes my hand as he leads me to an open booth to sit.

"Not gonna happen," he says firmly when a waitress brings us two menus.

"Evening, Dr. Bradley. How are you?" she flirts in a friendly manner, making me wonder if she means it or not.

I mean, if I wasn't such a jumbled mess over a bunch of inhuman men, *I* would flirt with him. Only a fool would pass up on the opportunity to be with someone as wonderful as Mark Bradley, but I'm definitely a fool.

A reckless one who came back.

Mark smiles at the woman politely, just like he did with the night nurse, not engaging with her much. In fact, he barely takes his eyes off of me—something the waitress notices. Her curious gaze tells me she doesn't know who I am, which is just fine with me. Growing up in a small town like Cleburne means gossip spreads faster than a wildfire, and anything that's meant to be a secret everyone knows about it.

"What will you have, hun?" the waitress asks me.

The man seated across from me winks in challenge.

"Chicken and waffles basket," I announce, internally making a face at the order.

The woman scribbles it down and walks off to get our drinks. Mark is staring intently at me, and I fidget nervously, making the vinyl of the booth squeak embarrassingly underneath me.

"What?" I wonder. Mark blinks, a confused look rolling across his features. "You're staring at me," I clarify.

"Sorry," he apologizes, running a hand through his thick, dark hair. "Kind of hard not to, though."

Now, I'm blinking in confusion.

"Um, what do you mean?"

A soft laugh tumbles from Mark's full lips.

"You never did realize just how gorgeous you are," he compliments, making me blush.

I try to shrug nonchalantly.

"Just another blue-eyed blonde," I murmur in response, and he immediately shakes his head.

"You're so much more than that—*so much more*," he whispers with husky fervor.

Tears sting my eyes, and I quickly duck my head before Mark can see their wet sheen under the bright, florescent lights of the diner. I don't deserve his adoration—I didn't back then nor do I now. At least back then, I tried to be honorable to him, to myself. Now, I can't say the same, not with dreams of monsters tying me to my bed and taking advantage of me.

"I've made you uncomfortable," he remarks sadly.

"No! You were complimenting me...and I was being rude. I just don't know what to say in response..."

"No, it's my fault," he sighs. "I said this was a friends' dinner, and I'm making a muck of it. Let's start over. Tell me about Australia."

There are no monsters.

I open my mouth to respond, but the waitress appears with our baskets of food. She sets one down in front of Mark, and then me, before setting down a jar of homemade syrup. I watch Mark drizzle it liberally over his waffles—and chicken. When he finishes, he passes the bottle over to me. I take it tentatively, still not sold on this whole chicken and waffles thing, but when in Rome, right?

Even though my old boyfriend claims this is just a friends' dinner, he's staring hungrily at my mouth as I lick a drop of syrup from my fingers. Blushing, I set the sweetener aside and dig in. Surprisingly, it's delicious—and I'm famished. Mark is still gazing intently at me, and I realize I'm making all sorts of inappropriate noises, hums, sighs, and groans of foody ecstasy. Panicked, I start blurting out things about my life Down Under. Mark listens intently, chewing slowly while I scarf my C and W down.

"How different is Australia from America?" he wonders, making me laugh.

"Like night and day!" I crow before listing the major differences between Oz and the States.

Mark's enchanted expression becomes pained.

"Oh, wow, that is pretty different. Do you like it there?" he probes.

"I love it there! I adore my job, my house—the whole country! Well, I do *not* love the spiders and the snakes, but it's really no different than Texas, right?" I chuckle.

Mark doesn't smile, though. He just looks... miserable.

"What's wrong?" I prod, knowing I shouldn't.

Deep down, I know the problem is *me*.

"I guess I was hoping that you'd say you miss home. That Australia wasn't where you wanted to be, and that you'd come back—*to stay*."

I swallow thickly.

This is why I shouldn't ask questions because I rarely want to acknowledge the answers.

"It's not that I don't like it here," I lie badly, trying to recover our earlier, easier banter. "But I have a life in Oz."

"You used to have a life here," he counters softly.

Thankfully, the waitress comes up to ask about dessert. Mark and I both pass—I mean, we had *waffles* with chicken. The air is electrically charged between the two of us as I pull out my purse to pay, but Mark stops me.

"I've got this," he says, handing the waitress some cash. "Thank you, keep the change," he tells her as I try to butt-in.

It's as if the woman never hears me as she walks away.

"I thought this was a "friends' dinner"?" I accuse.

"Friends can buy friends dinner," Mark smirks.

Tossing my hands up in vexation, I stomp after the irritatingly good-looking man as he strides out of the diner into the sunset. *Texas does have some pretty amazing sunsets.*

"Wait!" I call.

Mark pauses, looking over his shoulder at me, the gold flecks in his eyes smoldering at me.

"Ready to go home?" he queries as blandly as possible, but I can tell he wants to say something else entirely.

This time, I wisely abstain from asking those questions that open cans of worms. Instead, I ponder Mark's words.

Am I ready to go home?

It's finally come down to this moment. I must choose

whether coming this far is enough, or will I return to Australia with regrets? Do I need to actually step foot in my childhood home to feel like I've properly exorcised my demons, or was coming back about assuaging my guilt?

Have I even done that, really?

Truthfully, I came here to exonerate myself—liberate my heart and soul—but instead, I think I just dug up the shackles that tie me to this place with no hope of ever breaking free of them.

Or the monsters who placed them on me.

Thankfully, Mark saves me from my internal crisis.

"Or we could get a nightcap?" he suggests. "That's something I can say we've never done together."

My lips curl upward at his words.

"No, we were too young to go to the bars... and too nerdy," I joke.

He laughs.

"Yes, we were," Mark agrees.

He was the valedictorian of our class, and I was the salutatorian.

I nibble my lower lip, pondering my choices. Mark insists dinner was between friends, but his eyes tell another story. If I go to a bar with him, he might get the wrong idea—worse, I don't want him to think I'm leading him on—but I just don't know if I'm ready to face that house yet.

"One drink," I finally decide.

How much can one drink hurt?

CHAPTER

FIVE

Turns out one drink can be very dangerous—especially when one turns into four.

Mark takes me to Old Joe's, a popular bar that was here when I was a kid. It must still be doing well because it's packed when we arrive. The inside is loud and smoke-filled because Texans don't care about the no smoking rules. I follow Mark, my eyes wide, as people stop to shout out greetings—people I recognize.

And who recognize me back.

Whispers begin to buzz around me, and I feel the weight of everyone's stares. My breathing becomes quick and shallow, my palms slick with sweat. Mark casually sidles into a stool at the bar.

"Hey, Jason, can I get a Lone Star? Lexie, what would you like?"

I don't answer because I'm having a full-on panic attack. The world around me gets fuzzy, and my throat slowly—painfully—constricts inward until all airflow is cut off. Bright spots dance into my vision, and I know I'm going to pass out. Just when I'm ready to tumble into the darkened abyss, a clawed hand reaches out from my memories. A pair of glowing eyes swims into view, and I know that while I don't want to remain conscious, being unconscious is much more dangerous.

That's when the monsters in my mind run unchecked.

Surprisingly, it's a human embrace and familiar cologne that brings me back to the present. My cheek is plastered to someone's chest and tears are raining down my face —my own.

"Alexis, can you hear me?"

It's Mark, stalwart as ever.

"Yes," I croak, coming fully back into my body, gulping down air in almost vicious inhales. "I'm... having... an attack."

I manage these words in gasps, but feel Mark's arms tighten around me.

"Ok, let me get you out of here," he murmurs, but I tip back my head to stop him.

"No, I just... need a moment."

Mark frowns.

"Lex, you need to be somewhere quiet—"

"Usually. I'm no stranger to these, but tonight I need to address my trigger."

Concern and doubt are etched in equal measure in Mark's features. I can tell he wants nothing more than to whisk me away, but I have to do this. If I can't address this one, small fear in the face of the many that I have, how can I ever expect myself to conquer my demons? The honest truth is I won't be able to, and so, I turn back resolutely to the bar, at the man who once dated my best friend on-and-off. I can't look at him without thinking of her.

And I can't think of her without remembering the incident.

"Hi, Jason. Can I please have a vodka tonic with lime, please?"

He looks uneasily between me and my old boyfriend, unsure if he should take my order, but Mark nods, sitting down onto the stool. I follow suit, folding my hands in front of me serenely, practicing on my breath as my therapist taught me. I know everyone saw my meltdown, but I refuse to act like there's anything wrong with what transpired. There's nothing wrong with anxiety—and Lord knows I have enough of it to fill this entire bar to the brim—but I refuse to let it go uncontrolled.

It can rule me, or I can rule it.

Jason brings me my drink, as well as Mark's, and I sip it daintily. The alcohol burns a fiery path down to my stomach where it incinerates some of my inhibitions. Each swallow brings more ease to the situation. At some point, I order another vodka tonic; Mark frowns, but follows suit. For a time, neither of us speak, and I welcome the silence both between us and inside my head. For once, my mind is blissfully quiet. I forgot how mellowing booze can be. When I first fled the States to Australia, I buckled down to work.

After a few years, the guilt became too much, and I started to join my colleagues after hours. Like others before me, I used liquor to numb the pain, but after too many one-night stands and a pregnancy scare, I woke up to the reality of my life. I was walking a dangerous path. I traded in the booze for breathing, the bars for therapy, and haven't been in one since.

Until tonight.

I wasn't an alcoholic, so I don't consider being here a relapse. Still, I recognize that being here isn't the best decision—coming back in general probably wasn't—I tended to make poor choices when I drank. *I doubt tonight is any differ-*

ent. Alcohol loosens all my inhibitions and makes me needy, a terrible pairing, in my opinion. Four drinks in and I can feel the familiar loneliness creeping out.

Most days, I can keep that shit locked up. I can't be friends with anyone—they'd never understand—but Mark is a completely different ball game. He symbolizes the time before the incident. Mark represents everything I wish my life could be here—*normal*. Dating him was normal. Lusting after him was normal. Confiding in him was normal. But nothing about me is normal, maybe it never was.

And that's my biggest fear rearing its ugly head—I will never be able to fit in, not here, not anywhere.

I raise a hand for a fifth drink, but Mark firmly stops me.

"No more," he slurs, making me giggle.

Dr. Big and Hunky can't hold his liquor any better than me!

"One more," I attempt to negotiate, but a terrifying frown mars Mark's gorgeous features. "Ok, no more," I pout.

"You're sexy as fuck when you stick out your bottom lip. Makes me want to bite it while I spank you," he purrs in a low voice that only reaches my ears.

My mouth pops open in a shocked O of surprise at a side of Mark I didn't know existed. To be fair, we were both each other's first time. When you're that young, you don't really know what you're into—you haven't tried anything to know what you like. At eighteen, I had only one sexual proclivity, and I tried to keep that boxed up tighter than the fact I kept nightly company with monsters.

"I like being spanked," I blurt out loudly, earning a chuckle from Jason on the other side of the bar.

"Sounds like you need to take this somewhere else," he suggests.

Seeing him now through the rosy glasses of drunkenness, I don't feel the fluttering dread as I did before. I ponder his words—maybe Mark and I *should* take this elsewhere. I lean into Mark, breathing in his scent; it's both comforting and arousing.

"Wanna get out of here?" Before Mark can answer, I add, "Tell me 'no'."

He looks at me like I'm insane, but does as I've directed.

"No," he rumbles, and I immediately stick out my bottom lip again in an exaggerated move. Mark sucks in a breath at the sight before growling, "Let's. Go."

Mission accomplished.

Something in my brain cautions me that this isn't what I want, but then I catch sight of Mark walking off to talk to someone, his ass on perfect display in the tailored suit he's wearing. My brain shuts up. Mark comes back, his face set in determined lines.

"Come on. A friend is going to give us a ride since we aren't fit to drive."

That statement alone should remind me I'm not in a place to make other decisions, as well, but my brain is fixated on Mark's backside. *Does the man do Brazilian butt-lifts? Why is that thought oddly erotic?* I envision Mark on his back, clenching his ass together, before lifting up and down —*and I'm riding him reverse-cowgirl.*

It's definitely time for me to go.

I need a cold shower to douse out the insanity.

Trusting Mark implicitly, I climb into a stranger's backseat. I don't even attempt to see who's driving—better to pretend we don't know one another in case it *is* someone who knows me. Mark saves me from further embarrassment by sitting up front. It doesn't cool the fire raging in my blood, but puts it on simmer. I spend the fifteen-minute trip thinking of all the dirty, messed up things I want monsters to do to me, but can have Mark do instead. He's finally going to scratch my infernal itch, and nothing can stop us now...

Except pulling up in front of my childhood home.

"What the fuck?!" I shriek in horror.

Both men in the front seat swivel to face me, their faces mirroring one another's shock at my words.

"What's wrong?" the driver asks.

I glance at his face, registering it as one I do know, but it doesn't matter in this moment. All my attention—all my panic—is funneled into where I am. Every window is aglow on the main floor, illuminating where all my nightmares start and end. I spent twenty-some hours on a plane pumping myself up for this moment, only to realize I can't do it.

"You know, I should get back to the hospital—just in case."

Mark's eyes flash with hurt at what he thinks is a rejection of him—of us—but it's really being here. It's a trigger I can't handle.

"Your dad said you were going to say that. He doesn't want you to put yourself out just for him. Trust me, those waiting room chairs are not comfortable. I've slept in them before."

A truck pulls up behind us, the headlights making me wince as brightness fills the car. The driver who brought us hops out like his ass is on fire, gets into the truck, and both disappear into the night.

"Erm, I'm confused," I confess, my drunk brain only slightly more sober and alert because of where I am.

"This is my car, Lex," Mark sighs.

"Oh. I didn't notice. I was thinking about...other things."

Mark snorts.

"Did coming here ruin those thoughts?"

"Sort of," I admit.

He stares into the inky abyss of the sky above.

"Well, we can't go anywhere now until one of us sobers up completely."

His accurate assessment makes me tremble. Even though Mark is lit, he still notices. Unbuckling his seatbelt, he twists and crawls over the center console to sit beside me. It brings back memories of when we first started dating and would make out in his parents' car because he didn't have one of his own at the time.

"Breathe, Lexie. It's going to be ok," he vows, reaching up to cup my face between his hands.

I open my mouth, prepared to list all the reasons why it's *not* ok, but Mark's lips swallow the words. It's a long, slow, leisurely kiss meant to ignite my passion from before. My body hums with electric awareness, and I don't know if it's because of this kiss or because of what I think's inside the house—and the things I've dreamed of them doing to my body. Mark shifts, and I take the opportunity to reposition myself in his lap.

He's sitting in the center with his long legs sprawled wide behind the front seats, giving me ample room to sink into him. My knees box him in on either side, and my hips swivel of their own accord. The wetness between my legs quickly dampens my thong and thin leggings. It will only be a matter of time until I'm soaking his business suit, too. An almost inhuman growl escapes Mark's throat, making me pause.

The sound reminds me of *them*.

"We're going inside," Mark announces. "I refuse to do this in the backseat of my car. We're not eighteen anymore."

"I can't go in there."

"Yes, you can."

"NO, I CAN'T! I'm not strong enough!"

Mark briefly closes his eyes before reopening them, the brown nearly eclipsed by the black of his pupils.

"Alexis Stanton, you were one of the strongest, most beautiful people I'd ever met. I doubt that's changed in twelve years. You can do this. *We* can do this—together."

"B-b-but—" I stammer inanely.

"No 'buts' about it. If you want this," he snarls gently, pushing up roughly and grinding against me, "then we're going inside."

My lips pucker at his words, sealing the deal without me realizing it. Mark grabs my shoulders, tipping me to the side until I'm lying across his lap. His hard cock pokes my stomach as a swift hand comes crashing down against my ass. My gasp of surprise echoes around us, followed by my low moan of need. I wiggle in anticipation, hiking my backside upward in invitation, but Mark doesn't spank me again. I crane my head to the side, the tell-tale, instigator pout already on my lips to encourage more fun, but then I see his face. It's resolute.

No more spanking unless we go inside.

I pull away, shoving at the thick blond waves of hair flopping in my face. Closing my eyes and pursing my lips, I give a sharp nod.

"Ok," I reluctantly agree. The smile Mark beams at me is breathtaking. "But not in my room!" I quickly add.

That's an absolute dealbreaker, spanking or no spanking.

"I'll settle for a couch," Mark teases, opening the left rear door and holding out a hand for me to take.

Deciding if he thinks I'm strong enough, I slide out of the car. Still holding hands, I let Mark lead me onto the porch and into a house filled with the dust of my past. Once inside, I stare at him instead of my surroundings. In the glow of light, I see the boy I once knew inside of the man now before me. He knows what he wants, but doesn't want to push me too hard. Neither of us should be doing this—not in our current state and not in this house—but I need him to help me forget.

To erase the old memories and replace them with new ones.

Better ones.

I'm one hundred percent using this man to help me get through the next few hours with every intention of leaving him again. It broke his heart when I left before, and a nicer, better person would run away, but I'm not better.

I'm broken.

Mark and I come together like two comets crashing into one another. There's an urgency in our actions—him as if he can erase me leaving and me as if I can erase coming back. Both of us have an agenda, solving our own problems in very wrong ways that we'll likely regret later.

I guess I'm not the only one who's broken here.

CHAPTER SIX

Mark leads me to the living room where the couch sits in nearly pristine condition. My dad rarely spent any time in here when I was a kid, preferring to relax in the den off the kitchen—a habit he's obviously maintained. I try not to let any other thoughts invade my head, but I find myself distracted by every little sound...

What if it's them?

Another growl from Mark has me jumping at the sound. Frustration mixed with passion and tenderness are written all over his face, as well as determination. Scooping me into a loose embrace, Mark twines his hands around my ass, squeezing to get my full attention, which is not firmly locked on him. He leans down to kiss me while slipping his hands inside my leggings, grazing my goose-bumped flesh as he shimmies my pants down my legs. Next, Mark tugs my shirt over my head until I'm only standing before him in a powder-blue lingerie set that matches my eyes.

"*Jesus fuck*," he moans, and I blink at the curse.

"Is something wrong?" I wonder hesitantly.

In answer, Mark sinks to his knees, clutching my thighs

tightly and burying his nose between them. I gasp in surprise, falling forward a bit. The movement spreads my legs wider, and Mark dives right in, his teeth and tongue pushing past the delicate lace of my thong. Eventually, his hands push the fabric away, baring my pussy to his gaze and the warm night air filtering through an open window. Mark licks his lips and they glisten in the light, shiny from *me*.

"More," Mark demands.

The single word makes me tremble, reminding me of a green-eyed monster with a penchant for one-word phrases.

Snapping my attention back to Mark, I realize he's guiding me to the couch, where he gently pushes me back onto it. I land, sprawled and exposed—just like he intended. Mark dives between my legs, his mouth feasting at my center, igniting me faster than gasoline to a flame. Fisting his hair, I pull him closer for more, never wanting him to stop. The way he uses his tongue...

It makes me wonder how it would feel if it were longer.

Jerking abruptly, I bring my hand to my mouth, biting down hard on the fleshy part of my palm until I taste blood, but it does nothing to dissipate the rambling of my thoughts —which are not preoccupied with Mark's teeth nibbling around my clit, the blunt edge creating an intense contrast of pain and pleasure.

What if his teeth were even sharper?

When I look back down, I don't see Mark's face peering up between the whites of my thighs, but another all-together monstrous one graced with glowing eyes, a flattened nose, pointed teeth, and an impossibly long tongue —*shoved inches deep in my pussy*. An evil smirk curls the monster's lip just as he pierces me with a sharp fang. Instead of acute agony, all I feel is a powerful lust that blasts through my body like an inferno as I shatter and come, screaming out into the night.

When I finally descend from my high, it's Mark's face I see grinning at me. Shame slams into me like a freight train —*what is wrong with me?* Mark is one of the best-looking men I've ever met, but here I am, envisioning something out of a horror movie eating me out—*and getting off to it!* Unclipping my bra, I cast it aside before pulling Mark forward onto the couch.

"I thought you were going to spank me?" I challenge to derail my thoughts.

Mark's golden brown eyes twinkle. In a flash, I'm sprawled across his lap once more, and his hand is crashing down against my backside. Although my leggings are thin, they still provided a barrier back in the car; now, it's flesh upon flesh, the loud slapping sound echoing around us. I wiggle a bit as Mark's hand bites into my skin harder and harder.

"Mmmm," he hums, the sound one of the most erotic I've heard beside a hiss. "I love how pink you turn."

I squirm under his administrations and his words.

"Want me to stop?" he queries.

Smirking into his thigh, I turn my head so he can see my face and pout—before turning back and playfully nipping the inside of his leg.

SMACK!

I would laugh in victory, but the delicious sensations overtaking my body control all my thoughts. Mark spanks me a few more times before rubbing my ass and slipping a finger between my cheeks, sliding easily below into my dripping pussy. He finger fucks me into another orgasm, and this time, I scream his name to remind myself who made me come. Sitting up in his lap, I lick his fingers clean, drawing another deep growl from his chest.

"Lay back," he barks, sliding off the couch to yank his pants and boxers down before rolling on a condom.

"I'm on the Pill," I tell him in a husky whisper.

"One day, I'll fuck you bare, but not tonight," Mark promises.

His words make me shiver, so dirty in comparison to his normal gentlemanly manners. I love it. Once ready, he surges forward, nestling his impressive length right where I want him most.

"Are you ready?" he questions with worry, pausing at my threshold.

In answer, I lift my hips while gripping his and thrusting upward, impaling myself on him. Mark groans, a dark, delicious sound that makes my pussy clench tightly around his cock. He starts fucking me in earnest, burying his neck in my throat while I stare at the ceiling in rapture. Even without him playing with my clit, I can feel the familiar tingle down below, indicating another orgasm. He might actually be a sex god. Just as I'm about to come, a faint noise sounds above, drawing my attention.

Scratch, scratch, scratch.

My breath comes out in part gasp, part moan as Mark continues to slam into me hard and fast. The scratching sounds return, louder and harder, alerting me as it was intended because the room directly above this is mine. Mark shifts, his dick kissing the part deep inside of me that lights up my world. I cry out involuntarily, and I swear I hear the familiar tap of monstrous claws against the floor.

They're there, listening.

Waiting.

My throat constricts in fear, but it fuels my lust even more, ramping up my pleasure until I'm nearly blinded with it. Like all those years ago, I know my monsters are feeding into my needs. I close my eyes, envisioning shadowy hands trailing all over my body while Mark fucks me. When I shatter, my scream easily carries into the night, and to them. Mark comes seconds later, his moan equally loud, and I tremble.

What have I done?

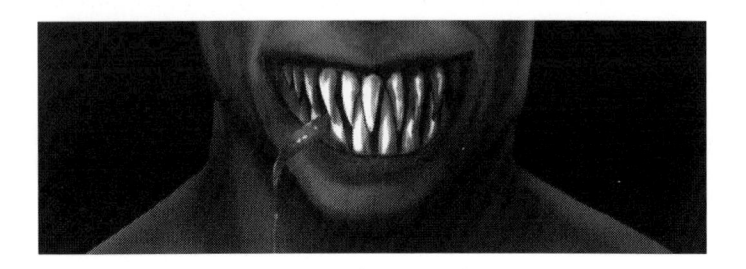

When I wake up, Mark's gone.

Next to my head on the couch pillow is a note explaining there was an emergency at the hospital. I squint into the bright, late morning sunlight that's streaming through the living room window as I grab my phone to see what time it is. Flashbacks of last night start filtering in through my mind.

What Mark and I did—*and who it woke.*

Gripping my hands tightly, I rock slightly back and forth, trying to convince myself that I'm mistaken. The scratching sound that I heard was definitely just a mouse this time, and my orgasm had nothing to do with monsters. I stare sightlessly around the living room that's been unchanged for over a decade. Obviously, my dad hasn't moved on.

Am I just like him, stuck in the perpetual rut of my own memories and fears?

I said that I came back here to face them, but have I?

Sitting up straighter, sucking in a cleansing breath, I acknowledge that I want answers. In the light of day—*when monsters can't get me*—I can be brave enough to search for what I yearn to know. I need to know what happened twelve years ago that night in my room.

I need *closure*.

Resolutely, I surge off the couch, past the fireplace mantle lined with pictures that my mom had placed there eons ago, towards the staircase leading to the second floor. Trailing my hand up the banister, I tiptoe upstairs. The door to my dad's room is open, another example of the man clinging to the past—*one where my mom's still in it*. Everything is the same. Her clothes are still in the closet. The last book she read is still on the nightstand with the same glass of water she used to sip from.

Seeing this is a testimony of the dedication Dad has to his memory of my mom—which means when I leave their room and walk down the hall to the door at the end, I know what I'm going to find inside. Slowly, agonizingly, I turn the knob to my bedroom and ease the door open. Inch by inch, it's revealed to me, but unlike my parents' room, this one hasn't been inhabited in well over a decade. The time shows in the dust that coats everything and the opened curtains that have been yellowed by the sun's rays.

Peering about, it's obvious I was a little princess, and my room was a fairytale come true for when I was a little girl—but that fairy tale turned into a never ending nightmare. The space is dominated by a large bed complete with a pastel pink canopy and a white dresser to the right next to the closet. When I moved, I picked furniture as far from what I had growing up as possible—this ensured it couldn't hide some of the most terrifying creatures anyone could imagine. Flashes of their glowing eyes, sharp teeth, and long, curved fingernails float across my mind. I close my eyes and gasp, stumbling back out of the room.

"No!" I shout out loud.

I didn't come this far to run away.

Stealing my spine, I force myself to walk back into the room. The streaming, bright morning light helps to calm my nerves. I know they're not here *now*, but they'll return. There's not a shadow of a doubt in my mind that they were here last night, but I try to convince myself it's just my fear and imagination getting the better of me. They couldn't have been here... I was just thinking of them when I came.

Which is even worse.

I run a hand through my disheveled hair, my lips twisting in disgust.

Who would fantasize about these monsters, these beasts?

Breathing evenly as possible, I step back into the room and look around again, reacquainting myself with things I have long forgotten. On the other side of the closet is a cork board pinned with all my hopes and dreams through my poems and artwork. Below it is a desk still cluttered with homework, awards, notes, and a long-forgotten stuffed animal that Mark had given me. My eyes bounce from one thing to another, feasting on the memories. I turn, skipping over the bed, my gaze landing on a chair in the corner and a familiar sweatshirt tossed carelessly over it. The sight is enough to bring me to my knees, and my vision goes hazy. I realize then I was mistaken.

I thought I could do this—but I'm not strong enough.

CHAPTER

SEVEN
15 Years Ago

A sound rouses me from my sleep, a light scratching that seems to be coming from underneath my bed. It's not odd to find a mouse or two in the attic during the colder months, or maybe even the basement—I do live in an old farmhouse, after all—what's odd is that it's in *my* bedroom in the dead of summer.

Scratch, scratch, scratch.

Moving quickly, I turn on my bedside lamp and lean over my bed, but nothing is there. *Damn, that's one quick mouse.* I scan the narrow area one more time, asserting that nothing is lurking under my bed, wondering where the little, furry monster scurried off. Suppressing the urge to shudder, I roll back onto my bed. I don't mind mice *as long as they're outside*. Biting my lip, I take a quick look to my closet, wondering if it was small enough to shimmy under the closed doors. I really don't want it pooping on my carpet or tearing up my clothes.

Nothing.

It's like the thing vanished into thin air.

My ears strain to pick up any sound of where the creature might have gone, as I climb back into bed. Minutes trickle by and I don't hear anything. Giving up, I flick off my lamp and try to go back to sleep. Unfortunately, I'm too attuned with my surroundings now—too awake, alert, and on edge. My panic over the mouse gives way to other thoughts and worries, mainly my parents. They've been fighting a lot, but not in a normal manner. Instead of blowing up in one another's faces, it's heated, angry whispers—like two angry barn cats hissing at one another. They pretend like everything is ok, but mom is gone a lot these days.

None of us talk about where she's going.

I've tried, but of course, my mom and dad only deflect my questions. It's hard to reassure myself that they're ok —*that our family is ok*—when they barely even talk to me. It seems like they are constantly bickering, but then I blink, and the two of them are clinging to one another like they are the only two people left on this planet. I can't make any sense of it and have withdrawn into my own head—it's less painful there.

But only barely.

The scratching sound returns, abruptly yanking me from my raw thoughts. Glad for the distraction, I slowly and quietly ease myself near the edge of my bed, using my comforter to keep me anchored on top when I lean over. Gripping the frame, my torso hangs suspended with only my legs still atop the mattress. My long, blond hair is pulled into a messy bun and doesn't brush the floor—which would have alerted the mouse before I could see it.

Inch by agonizing inch, I lower myself until my eyes can barely peek under my bed, my core muscles straining at both my pace and position. From my upside-down perch, I scan the area for the four-legged, hairy menace, but instead, a pair of large, wide set, glowing red eyes meet mine. My scream rends the air as I catapult myself upward and back into the center of my bed. From down the hall, I can hear my parents scrambling to get to me. When they enter the room and I tell them what I saw, they regard me with a mixture of sadness and pity. I didn't realize they thought it was an attempt for attention—a cry for help—one they would be counseled to ignore.

So the next time I screamed, no one came, and I was at the mercy of a monster.

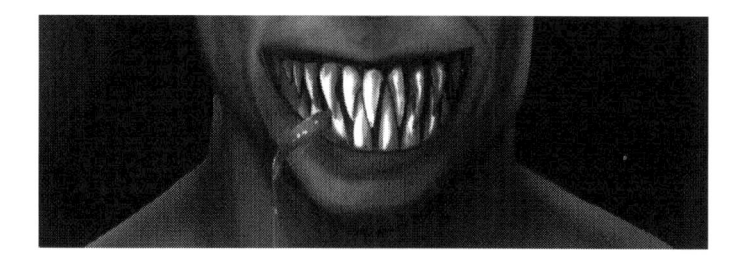

I gasp as I come to, my memory so vivid that it feels like I've flown back in time. If I keep my eyes closed, I can see his fiery, red eyes, feel his clawed grasp, inhale his earthy scent, and hear his husky laugh. Bile threatens to erupt from my throat, the acrid taste making me wince. I cough, trying to dislodge the flavor as well as the urge.

Funny thing about memories—*they often are more potent than real life, trapping you in the nightmare of your past where you can never escape.*

I exhale, powerfully thrusting myself into the present. I look around trying to recall what happened when my gaze lands once more on the sweater—Roxy's sweater. The pink plaid sears a pattern of remembrance and guilt across my heart. I pick up the soft flannel, dusty from time, and rub it against my face.

God, I miss Roxy.

A book underneath the shirt catches my eye, and I realize it's my diary. I hadn't thought about this thing in ages. I pick it up, flipping through the entries, noting the last one made was April, twelve years ago, a day before the most life changing event ever happened in my life. I didn't write in my diary after that.

Hell, I didn't even return to my house.

I spent the remaining month and a half of my senior year in a mental institution, and no coaxing by either of my parents could get me to come back onto the property. During the summer months, I elected to live in a halfway home, working my ass off. When I finally made enough money, I bought a one-way ticket to Australia, where I got a job and I never looked back.

I was given the diary for my fifteenth birthday, shortly before my life became a living nightmare. The first few months of entries I read reflect the external worry for my mother, my parents, and their marriage. The entries that follow show a slow descent into the hysteria of my mind, of the constant fear I lived in, and the absolute isolation that encased me when no one believed me. I try not to be bitter, understanding why my parents didn't listen to me, but it still hurts, nonetheless. I flip to an entry marked fourteen years before.

Today marks the one year anniversary that a monster started terrorizing me. It's been three hundred and sixty-five days of hell. I can barely sleep. I can barely function. Every night, he's there. It started out as just one of them, a constant companion whenever my room got dark. I finally caved and asked my parents for a nightlight, but both think it might disrupt my sleep—hilarious considering I barely sleep as it is. For the first few months, the monster with red eyes stalked me, scratching his nails on my wooden floor. When I showed my parents, they said it was just mice and put down traps. My mom and dad don't understand how they always went off, but there were never any mice. The monster liked to toy with me, setting them off at night to frighten me more. Eventually, he stopped hiding underneath my bed, slowly creeping out on moonless nights. A shadowy phantom lurking in the corners of my room, staring at me—watching, assessing—keeping me up all night. I fall asleep during school, and my grades have plummeted. My parents think I'm being rebellious and going through a phase, but no matter how dark the bags under my eyes get, nothing convinces them of the truth. One night, I woke up to find the red-eyed monster in the corner of my room—but he wasn't alone. Next to him was another monster, this one with glowing yellow eyes. Every night, they become more and more familiar, stepping out of the shadows, invading my every waking thought. I've tried sleeping in different places around the house, but always wake up in my room. Did the monsters bring me back, or did I just sleepwalk there?

Rereading the words, a chill skitters down my spine. It's been fourteen years since I wrote that, and I *still* have no answer. Flipping through entries, I pause at one dated six months from the one I just read. Even before I glance at the words, I know this marked a turning point in my life.

April 16th

These monsters are not just shadows; they have solid forms. For some reason last night, they seemed more vibrant—more tangible—and as they became more solid, they stepped out of the shadows of my room. Slowly, they crept forward to the foot of my bed where they loomed over me, monstrously large. The one with red eyes reached out and touched me. I can still feel his hand on my ankle warm, large and rough, as if calloused. It was so big that it easily encircled my leg. I opened my mouth to scream, but no sound came out—that is, until the yellow-eyed one stepped forward, his eyes locked on mine. My body shook convulsively at the intent glistening in those glowing depths. All the while, the other monster never let go of me. Finally, after an eternity, the neon-eyed one opened his mouth, his lips stretching into a victorious grin filled with razor sharp teeth, and said, "Alexis."

I stop reading. I'll never forget the scream at hearing one of them speak. In nearly two years of them visiting, never once had they said anything to me—or touched me. *Why then?* More unanswered questions that haunt me. My parents came to my room that night; I woke them both up with my shrill shriek of fright. It was then they decided something *was* wrong. Of course, it wasn't the monsters I told them about. No, they feared for my mental stability—the pressure that school, my future, and other *unspoken* things were causing me. They took me to the doctor who gave me sleeping pills for a short time. At first, they worked, and I was blissfully ignorant if any monsters came to visit me at night, but they still came in my dreams—turning them into nightmares. My sleep was restless, but at least I was getting some.

That is until one fateful night thirteen years ago when a third monster appeared.

CHAPTER EIGHT

A text brings me out of my reverie. It's from Mark, and I wonder when he programmed his number into my phone. Of course, after the intimacy we shared last night, do I have any right to be upset that he did add it? It's not like I kept my screen locked or anything. I tap the message open, wondering if things are going to be awkward between us, but welcome the distraction when his words register.

Get to the hospital immediately. Your dad's going back in for surgery.

My throat constricts at these words, trapping the air there and making it so I can barely swallow. I desperately want to message back, wondering what's happening, but know that Mark is busy—*he might even be saving my dad's life.* The fastest way I can get to the hospital is to get an Uber. It takes a bit for the driver to pick me up since it's coming from a neighboring town, and I wait outside impatiently.

The hospital is thirty-five minutes from the house, but by the time the Uber picks me up and delivers me, it's been well over an hour since I opened up Mark's text. I rush to the second floor where the nurse from the other day greets me.

"Hi, I got a text message from Mark, er, I mean Dr. Bradley about my dad being in surgery?"

"Hello, Miss Stanton! I'm sorry, but your father's still in surgery. If you would like, there's a waiting room just down the way where you can sit."

"Is there any way I can talk to Dr. Bradley?" I ask a bit frantically.

"I can forward a message to his pager that you're here, but he's filling in for another doctor who's out today and is extremely busy."

I nod, my hands twisting together in worry.

"My dad... is he—"

The nurse cuts me off.

"I'm sorry, Miss Stanton, I can't say anything because I genuinely don't know."

"Can you tell me what you do know?" I prompt.

"Of course! This morning, your father's vitals started to decline rapidly. They hooked him up to a machine, found out it was his heart, and immediately rushed him into surgery."

"Is it safe to have open heart surgery that quickly back-to-back?"

"It happens more frequently than you realize," the nurse reassures, and I relax a little.

"Oh, ok, so it's alright?"

The nurse opens her mouth and then closes it. She doesn't say one way or the other, but I'm happy to live in ignorant bliss—*I'm extremely adept at pretending everything's ok when it's not.*

"Can you please tell me when I can go see him?" I ask.

The phone rings, distracting her, and she gives me a brisk nod in response before answering the call. I wave to her, pointing that I'm going to go sit in the waiting room before walking into the empty room. Another hour and a half passes, and my mind wanders back to my diary. Against my will, the memories flare to life, and I'm thrown back to the night I met the third monster.

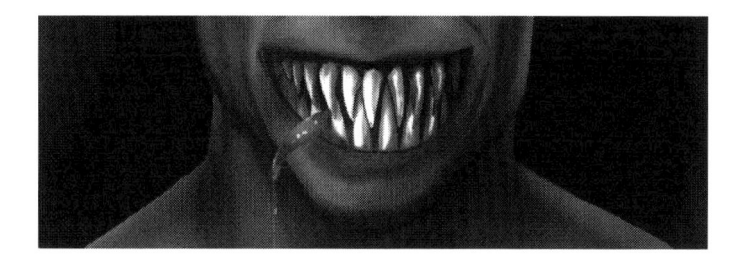

13 Years Ago

In the six months since the yellow-eyed one spoke to me, I've come to know the two monsters that terrorize me—although, I use that word loosely. Indeed, they do terrify me, but they don't harm me. *They're ever watchful, as if they're waiting, but for what?* They speak English, the language heavily accented as if they can't get the words around their long, pointed teeth and their /s/ are hissed, like a snake. I've learned their names, too. The red-eyed one is Xhoshad, spelled in a foreign way I'm not familiar with, and the yellow-eyed one is Nerazi.

By this time, I've completely cut myself off from the world around me. I only have a handful of friends—it's hard to pretend to be normal when you're not—my best friend, Roxy, and my boyfriend, Mark. They don't seem to mind that I'm a basket case.... *then again, they don't know.* I've never told them about what goes on at night and the monstrous men that visit me—who've become my nightmarish friends even. I love Roxy and Mark, but there's something so liberating being able to tell these monsters anything. I went from fearing them to forming some weird bond where I can tell them anything.

There's never any judgment; they just listen, and when the morning sun creeps in, they disappear.

I say that they're the demons, but in reality, it's like they're the exorcists for the ones inside of me. I even started to sleep again—*without my medication*. I feel safe, almost as if they are protecting me while I rest, until the third monster arrived. Nerazi told me his name is Seriq. This green-eyed monster never speaks, but stares at me with a rapt hunger that even a seventeen-year-old girl can recognize. His gaze awakens something dark inside of me—forbidden and unnatural.

Slowly, I stop fearing them and begin to fear myself.

Night after night, for a year, I suffer under Seriq's heated glances as something unfamiliar blossomed within me. It's so different from what I feel with my boyfriend. Mark is safe, but Seriq is fire—if I play with him, I'll go up in flames. I realize that I'm becoming a woman and the monsters know it. Seriq feeds into my emotions until I'm a ball of nervous tension and need—a need I don't know how to relieve. This goes on for half a year until my eighteenth birthday.

I come home to celebrate with my parents, but no one's home. Hurt and something darker churns inside of me. I don't know where they are—neither my mom nor dad talk to me anymore. I decide to celebrate on my own. Raiding my parents' liquor cabinet for the first time, I down a few shots of Patrón. It's nasty and burns like hell on the way down, but it incinerates all my pain, relaxing me completely.

Turning on some music, I make my way to my room, dancing sinuously to the beat. Once inside, I leave the lights on, not ready to confront the monsters who always expect me to talk about my feelings. I don't want to chat tonight, but after a few moments, I change my mind. Quickly flipping off the switch, I launch myself back onto the bed and continue to shake my hips. My hands skim over the exposed skin of my arms, legs, and stomach before I tuck my thumbs into my shorts.

A low growl is the only indication that my monsters are there and watching. Keeping my eyes tightly closed, I inch my shorts down, along with my underwear, exposing my virgin flesh to their glowing eyes. Later, I'll blame it on the liquor, but I knew everything over the last three years had been building up until this point. Touching myself like I do in the shower, I rub my fingers roughly over my clit before slowly stroking them inside of me—shallowly at first, but then deeper and deeper.

"More," a voice purrs greedily.

Nerazi, my two-faced monster who pretends to be civilized.

In answer, I fuck my pussy harder, imagining his long fingers tipped with deadly talons touching me in the same way while Xhoshad and Seriq watch. My lust ratchets up a notch at the thought, almost as if they're feeding it with merely their presence. A light touch on my leg startles me, and my eyes fly open to see the red-eyed monster hovering over me.

"Don't stop," he snarls, and I quickly obey.

Faster than lightning, I reach my peak. My breath explodes in raspy pants, and just as I come, another hand joins mine, long fingers digging into my welcoming warmth.

Against my will, my gaze locks with a vibrant green one. Seriq stares at me with a look akin to raw, territorial hunger, and as I shatter, he speaks for the first time ever, a single word.

Mine.

CHAPTER NINE

"Lexie?"

"Hmmm?" I hum, staring at the shadow of the lamp on the wall, wondering if it'll turn into something more.

"Alexis!" the voice repeats, this time sharply, and I look over to see Mark standing in the doorway of the waiting room.

"I'm so sorry; I must have been daydreaming."

Glancing down at my phone, I note that it's later in the afternoon and two more hours have passed since I last checked.

"Is my dad ok?" I wonder, quickly rising from the chair.

My back protests, aching from sitting still for so long as I stride toward Mark. He steps up to me, his face somber, and my heart takes a downward plunge at his expression.

"It's bad, isn't it?" I cringe, my shoulders sagging.

I acknowledge that I'm not returning home any time soon. My dad's going to need me, and I owe this to him to stay and care for him.

"Lex, your dad...." Mark trails off, unable to finish his

sentence. I wait patiently for him to tell me the bad news, wondering how long Dad's recovery will be. "Your dad died!"

Mark blurts this last part out, looking like he's about to be sick to his stomach. I blink in confusion, not comprehending his words.

"What?"

Taking a deep breath, Mark tries again, "Your dad passed away in surgery. I'm so sorry, Alexis. Dr. Frieden tried everything he could, but we couldn't staunch the bleeding—"

Mark's voice becomes fuzzy, and I stop hearing his words. My dad is dead. I just saw him yesterday, and he was fine! All those years of being gone—*of running away*—come crashing down on me, and for a second time today, my world goes black.

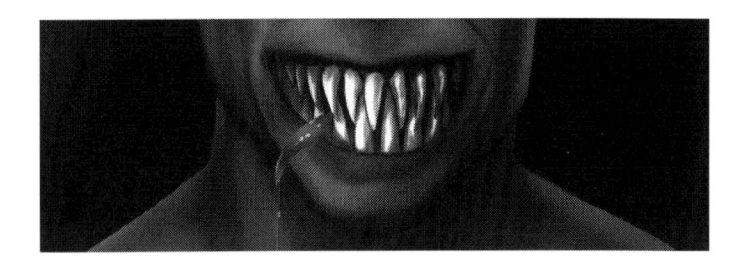

12 Years Ago

"I can't believe you *did it* with Mark."

A rush of emotions cascades over me at Roxy's excited words.

I can't believe I did it either.

The memory brings exhilaration, nervousness, and fear —*the latter of which I try not to focus on*. Mark and I had both been virgins, but there's still that worry I didn't do something right. It was an interesting experience for me. It was painful, of course—and nothing similar to the fireworks like that night when Seriq helped me orgasm—but amazingly meaningful to connect to another person in such a manner. The only thing marring the experience is my monsters.

Xhoshad, Nerazi, and Seriq.

In the three odd years that they've plagued me, I've run the gamut of emotions. My fear is mostly derived from *what* they are, but I can honestly say they've never hurt me. The three of them watch me in curiosity, amusement, and more recently, hunger. Occasionally, I see small flits of sadness when I talk to them about my parents, but for the most part, they are self-contained, their glowing eyes revealing nothing.

When I came home from my date with Mark after we had sex for the first time, my monsters were waiting there in the dark of my room. I didn't need to turn on my light because I no longer feared their presence—until I saw their eyes flashing with rage and a betrayal I didn't understand. For the first time in forever, I scrambled back, flipping the light switch up and vanquishing them to wherever they came from.

I slept with the lights on that night, alone and scared in my house. A few months earlier, my parents came forward with a revelation that would destroy our relationship. They weren't getting divorced—my mom was terminally ill and didn't want me to know. Now, she was so close to death, they had no choice but to tell me. I wonder how I could've been so blind not to see it and hated both my parents and myself. With my mother slipping fast and my dad preoccupied with taking care of her, I'd basically been left to fend for myself. Normally, I didn't mind—I had my monsters and they took care of me.

But they've never been pissed at me before.

"Lexie? Are you listening to me?" Roxy's voice calls.

"Erm, no, sorry," I apologize.

She rolls her eyes.

"Thinking about bumping uglies, huh?" she teases, waggling her eyebrows.

I toss back my head and laugh.

"*Please* stop calling it *that*," I chuckle.

"Well, I'm going to call it that because I'm jealous."

"Don't be jealous—it's not like anyone's stopping *you* from having sex," I point out.

"Sure they are!" she explodes. "I'm not in a meaningful relationship with anyone like you and Mark. I don't want to be another high school statistic that just gives it up to one guy after prom because that's what you're supposed to do your senior year."

I nod understandingly.

"You're right. I have something meaningful with Mark and get wanting the same thing."

"So, now I know your biggest secret," Roxy squeals, and I raise a brow.

My biggest secret?

Not even close.

"Um, yeah, I guess you do—who else to share it with other than my bestie?"

"I mean, I know Mark *knows*, duh, but it's not like you can talk to your parents about this."

Her words make me snort. Even if my parents were around, I still wouldn't tell them. I stopped confiding in my mom and dad when they didn't believe me—*couldn't believe me*—about monsters. They thought I was hallucinating due to stress and ingrained my fear that everyone secretly thinks I'm psycho. Their secrets and lies unraveled the string that held our family together until it was threadbare. Over the years, they just assumed I "got better" on my own—*they have no idea about the men that visit me at night in the dark of my room.*

I stare at my best friend, the weight of my secret pushing down on me harder than gravity.

"That's not my biggest secret," I explode in a whisper.

Roxy's eyes widen so much that she looks like a cartoon character.

"Was Mark not your first?!" she guesses.

"What? No! He totally was."

"Well, what could be bigger than *that*? And why haven't you told me?" she demands, crossing her arms over her chest.

"It's.... complicated," I hedge, and Roxy rolls her eyes.

"Everyone says that!"

"It's hard to explain—"

"Would you just spit it out!"

Seconds tick by while she gazes at me expectantly, and I build up the courage to confess.

"I have three men who are monsters that visit me every night in the dark," I finally blurt out.

Roxy's brows crinkle.

"You have.... *three monstrous men* that visit you every night?"

I nod solemnly.

"Like the bogeyman?"

I startle at her words.

Bogeymen—that's exactly what they are.

"That's a good name for them," I reflect.

"And you're sure you're not hallucinating?"

I glare at my best friend.

"No, I'm not *insane*. I told my parents when they first

started visiting me years ago. They eventually took me to go see a doctor and put me on medicine," I spit bitterly.

Roxy jolts.

"You never told me you were on medicine!"

"I was embarrassed. My parents think I'm a nut job—I didn't want my best friend thinking the same thing and leaving me."

She reaches out to touch my shoulder softly.

"I don't think you're crazy. If you tell me that these monsters are real—*then they're real*. All this time I thought it was your mom being sick that's made you so distant and tired.... It all makes so much more sense now!"

I look into Roxy's hazel eyes before throwing my arms around her and sobbing in relief. It suddenly feels like I'm a thousand pounds lighter from finally telling someone else my secret—but also to have someone believe me.

"I want to see them," Roxy demands.

"What?!" I gasp.

"I want to meet them," she repeats firmly.

"I don't know...." I trail off. "They're kind of mad at me, I think."

Roxy wrinkles her nose.

"Why?"

I shrug.

"I don't know. They've never been mad at me. It's just an impression I get, I guess."

"Well then, I *definitely* should be there with you. It doesn't sound safe."

"They would never hurt me!" I defend inanely, not sure how I know this.

"Do you have any proof of them?" Roxy wonders.

"No, not like you're thinking. There are scratches under my bed, but my parents say it's just mice, but I know it's from them. The only thing I have is my diary. You can read it if you want. I have been taking note of them for three years."

Roxy smirks.

"That's proof enough that you're not making it up—nobody puts that in their diary if it's not true."

"*Exactly!*" I laugh. "But my parents would never understand that."

"I do, and you're not going to face them alone. We'll figure out why they're mad and maybe what they want," Roxy declares.

I tip my head at this.

"What they want? Whaddya mean?"

My bestie gives me a keen look.

"Three men don't visit you for years in your room—in the dark of the night—and *not* want something."

My heart gallops in my chest at her words.

Was she right?

Did the monsters want something?

If so.... what?

CHAPTER TEN

The next two days pass in a blur of grief, no sleep, and keeping the lights on at all times in the room I'm staying in at the local bed and breakfast. I'd ordered my father's remains to be cremated and kept everyone at bay while I finalized everything to go back to Australia. I haven't spoken to Mark since he told me my dad died. It's like going back into my room unleashed a monstrous curse that's invading my life with its horrors.

What would be next?

A sharp knock on the door pierces through my mental musings. Warily, I get up and crack it open, expecting to find the sweet, old woman who runs the B&B, but find Mark instead. Sucking on my bottom lip, I internally debate what to do when he declares he's not budging from this spot until we talk. Sighing, I open the door wide and step back to let him in.

"How'd you find me?" I wonder tonelessly, making Mark snort.

"It's the only bed and breakfast in the town," he reminds, and I could smack myself for my own stupidity. Of course, he found me; I'm probably the only person staying here. I haven't seen any other cars, come to think of it. I suppose if I really was looking for anonymity, I should have holed up in a hotel a few towns over, but my brain isn't functioning at full capacity.

"I'm sorry—" I start, but Mark cuts me off.

"Alexis, you don't need to keep apologizing to me. I didn't come here to make you feel bad—I came to see if you were all right."

My fragile heart lurches at these words. I don't deserve somebody as good and kind as Mark in my life. I'm a terrible person who abandoned the people who loved me.

"I'm fine." I respond automatically, letting the lie hang in the air between us.

We both know it's not true; it's simply an involuntary response. Small talk that doesn't mean anything, once more proving what a terrible person I am because I can't even put forth the effort to give Mark more. But I'm so emotionally exhausted, I have nothing left to give him.

"Is there anything I can help with?" Mark offers awkwardly after we stand there in silence.

"No, I have everything arranged. My dad wanted to be cremated, apparently, but he has a headstone like my mom."

Mark nods thoughtfully.

"And the funeral?"

"Actually, I'm doing a memorial service, instead."

"Can I ask what time?" Mark prompts. "I would like to be there—for both you and your father."

My self-worth shatters at this, knowing I'm unworthy of his support.

"Of course," I croak hoarsely, profoundly moved at his endless kindness. "It's from twelve to two at Rosser Funeral Home."

Mark makes note of it on his phone, and silence descends between us again.

"So, I know you're thinking about going back--" he starts.

"I *am* going back," I correct firmly.

I can't let Mark get in his head that I might not be returning to Australia. There are no ifs, ands, or buts about it—*I can't stay here.*

"What about the house?" Mark wonders.

"I have someone taking care of that for me."

"And everything inside?" he prods.

Sighing heavily, I confess, "I'm going to put it all to auction and donate all the proceeds to the hospital."

"But wouldn't you want any of it?" he exclaims in surprise.

I shake my head. Mark will never understand. On the one hand, I do want the house and everything inside of it, but on the other hand, I want nothing at all.

Nothing that is linked to them.
Nothing that reminds me of them.
Nothing that could bring me back to them.

When I moved to Australia, I burned everything that came with me, and bought everything new. I wanted no ties and feared my monsters would follow me halfway around the world, but they didn't. I'm convinced that my room is their access point, and everything boils down to my childhood home.

"Alexis, that sounds—"

"Psychotic?" I smirk. "Yeah, I've heard that one before."

Mark shakes his head angrily.

"That's not what I was going to say! Don't put words in my mouth," he snaps.

I wince at his tone, but refuse to apologize. Whether he

realizes or not, that is what he was thinking—what everyone thinks, that I have a screw loose.

"So you're just going to stay a couple more nights?" Mark asks dully.

"No... I'm going to the memorial service tomorrow, and then, I have a flight leaving immediately after that."

Mark purses his lips and looks down before his brown eyes fly back to mine.

"What if I asked you to stay?" he pleads in earnest, making my stomach twist in guilt.

"Please, don't ask me that," I murmur dejectedly.

"But what about our night together? Didn't it mean anything to you?" Mark plows on, never one to give up.

I take a step back, needing to put space between us before I caved and gave into his every whim—both because I secretly crave it and to assuage my overflowing remorse. I contemplate his questions—*how do I answer them?*

Didn't he realize we were just using one another?

Is he delusional, or am I?

"Mark that was.... that was...."

I trail off again. I don't even have the words to express what happened between us because I don't have the heart to break his again. Except, that's exactly what I'm going to do tomorrow when I leave. Clearly, I am some kind of monster myself because I'm more than happy to run out on him again while refusing to give him the answers that he seeks. I know I should explain, but I can't bring myself to tell him what he deserves to know. Unfortunately for me and my battered heart, Mark isn't backing down. He grabs me by my shoulders, spinning me around, before clutching me tightly in his embrace.

"Tell me what happened!" he directs fiercely, and my

mind seizes when I realize he's talking about the night Roxy disappeared.

"You know what happened!" I cry. "You think I don't know that everyone whispers about me?"

Mark wipes the tears streaming down my cheeks gently with his thumbs.

"Lex, I know we're a small town, but I promise you, people weren't whispering things about you. *None of us* know what happened. One minute Roxy was here; the next, she was gone and then you were gone. Her disappearance was ruled as a runaway—"

"Roxy would *never* have run away," I counter flatly.

Mark swallows thickly.

"I know. Some people thought you had something to do with it." His words startle me, the thought never crossing my mind before this moment. "But it was ruled out early on that you were the culprit. Because there were no leads, it was decided that Roxy split. Her parents waited and waited but like you, they knew their daughter didn't run away. They died wondering what happened to their only child. Having Roxy go missing was... awful, but you leaving without ever saying goodbye? I still don't have the words to tell you how much that hurt. Please, don't do that to me again. I've been waiting for twelve years for you to return—to tell me what happened."

I pull out of his grasp, shaking all over.

"You won't believe me," I whisper.

"Try me," Mark counters gently.

A humorless laugh escapes from my throat.

He has no idea what he's asking for, I just hope he can handle the truth.

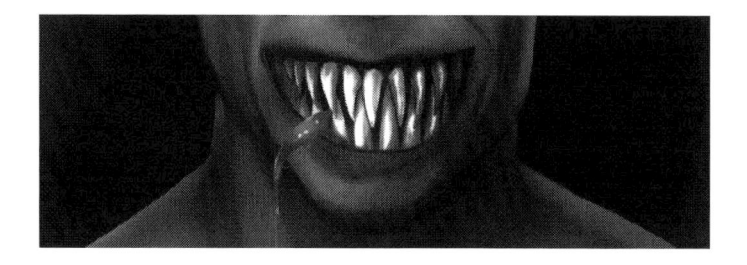

12 Years Ago
The Incident

"Where are you? I hope you're ok! Call me when you can."

I hang up my phone, wondering what's happened to Roxy. She was supposed to be here an hour ago. I nibble my lip, debating whether I should go over to her house, but know her parents do family things on the weekends—unlike my mom and dad. The caustic bitterness of that thought makes me both profoundly sad and furious.

When my parents first disclosed that my mom was sick, they told me they waited so long because they didn't want it to taint my youth. They wanted me to be carefree and happy—the opposite of how I felt inside. Both my mom and dad expressed the desire to normalize my teen years and spend as much time together. Ironically, both of them practically ignore me, too wrapped up in their problems.

I envy Roxy and the relationship she has with her parents. Her mom and dad make it a priority to spend time with her every weekend and eat all weekday meals together. I can't even remember the last time either of my parents *made* me a meal. At eighteen, I knew my way around the kitchen, or the drive-thru, if I was in a pinch, but it wasn't the same. This marked my fifth weekend in a row spent alone at my house.

If it wasn't for Mark, Roxy, and my monsters....
I would have no one.

I begged my dad to let me come with them when they went to the hospital, but my mom refused. She didn't want my last memories to be of her being sick. *Didn't she realize my last thoughts of her wouldn't be ones from my childhood ten years ago, but the neglect and grief of the ones from the past ten months?!*

Checking my phone to see if Roxy's texted me, I see it's past eight. Summer is coming, meaning my time with the monsters who live under my bed will rapidly become shorter, but it's getting dark enough now for them to come out. I wonder if I should wait for my best friend or confront them on my own. When another thirty minutes passes with no Roxy, I climb up the stairs to my bedroom. Slipping inside, I take a deep breath before flicking the light off. Immediately, three pairs of glowing eyes greet me.

"Why are you mad at me?" I demand before I lose my gumption.

Xhoshad, the red-eyed leader, comes forward, his shadow form slowly becoming more corporeal.

"You were supposed to be ours!" he snarls savagely, his sharp, white teeth gnashing together menacingly.

I stumble back, startled by his tone and words.

"I-I.... I don't know what you mean!"

"Yes, you do," Nerazi, the yellow-eyed trickster, counters mellowly, but I know his game.

He pretends to be the kind one, the gentle one; when in reality, he's waiting to pounce. I wisely keep my mouth shut, refusing to reply. Xhoshad comes forward, his red eyes gleaming brightly.

"How can you question us when we've smelled your lust and tasted your pleasure?" he demands, making me blanch.

"M-m-my pleasure?" I stutter. "How did you *taste* it?"

"Because your feelings are our food. Like humans, some things taste better to us than others, and your need is—"

"Delicious," Seriq hisses ferally.

I jump, spinning around to face him, but Nerazi sidles up to me, his shadow body taking solid form.

"And you gave that to some human boy!" he spits, letting his sweet façade fall to the wayside to show me the true monster that was underneath.

Comprehension dawns when I realize he's talking about Mark—they're angry that I slept with him....*because they wanted to sleep with me?* My mind turns the idea over.

"Your first time was supposed to be ours," Xhoshad adds, making me blush.

"You wanted my virginity?" I wonder.

"Yes, and more. *All of you*," Seriq growls, reaching for me.

Although I haven't panicked in their presence in years, I do so tonight, stumbling a bit until I find the light switch. Seriq's hand wraps around my wrist just as I turn it on, illuminating my room, and all three monsters instantly disappear. I've never learned where they go, but know they're always waiting in the dark.

A honking horn gets my attention, and I run to my bedroom window to see Roxy pulling up. I race downstairs to tell her what happened, but forget about Mr. Mittens. The damned feline bolts out the door into the night, and I curse his spotted ass. He's my mom's cat and my only responsibility while they're gone. She'll be devastated if anything happens to him—as will my dad. I wave to Roxy, pointing after Mr. Mittens, not daring to slow down. I finally catch up with him a quarter mile away, swearing obscenely.

Scolding him about chasing field mice, I haul his fluffy butt back, dumping him inside the dining room, calling for

Roxy. She hollers that she's in my room, and I shudder, yelling for her to come back down. After what just happened, I don't want to spend any time in my room, light or no light. I wait, but still she doesn't come down. Frowning, I shout again. Her voice is faint when she responds, meaning she's shut my bedroom door. My ears strain to hear her words, but when I do, my blood freezes.

She's turning off the lights.

"Roxy! STOP!" I bellow, but I know I'm too late.

Pounding up the stairs, her blood-curdling scream pierces the air and I stumble, tripping on the last step. Scrambling against the railing, I pull myself up and dash down the hall, throwing open my door, ready to confront the monsters who scared my friend....

Except, the room's empty.

I flip the light on and off.

On and off.

On and off.

But to no avail. The darkness never brings my monsters, or Roxy.

She's gone.

And they took her to punish me.

CHAPTER ELEVEN

"Monsters... took Roxy?"

Mark's voice isn't exactly incredulous, but I hear the skepticism in his question.

"Yes," I respond with conviction. "Monsters took Roxy—and not some fictional creation of my mind, but flesh and blood monsters."

"And you won't go back to your house because they're there now?"

"I think so. I think they're waiting for me in my room."

Comprehension dawns on Mark's face.

"That's why you refused to sleep in your room the other night."

I flinch, wondering how crazy I sound to him, but he wanted to know the truth—I merely obliged.

"Where did they take Roxy?"

Tossing my hands up in the air in frustration, I reply, "I've been trying to figure that out for twelve years! I have so many unanswered questions, I could fill a book."

Mark paces back and forth a short distance, his fingers rubbing his temples as he tries to think.

"So these monsters lived under your bed and only came out at night—like Bogeymen?"

"That's exactly what Roxy called them."

"That's what they sound like," he says in a disapproving tone.

"They helped me through a lot," I defend for some unknown reason.

"They stole Roxy and coveted you," Mark counters.

His words make me uneasy.

"They didn't "covet" me," I mutter.

"Really?" he challenges, but I don't respond. "Are they still there?"

I rub my arm in an attempt to comfort myself.

"I....I think so. I heard them the other night when we were.... um, you know," I hint.

"*Fucking,*" Mark deadpans in his deep voice.

My face flushes, the heat rising due to both his words and my mounting anger.

"Why are you mad at me?" I clip out, baffled, just as I was all those years ago.

"I'm not mad at *you*—I'm mad at them!"

"I know they took Roxy, trust me, that enrages me, but—"

Mark's biting laugh cuts me short.

"You don't get it. I'm.... *jealous* of these monster fucks," he confesses. "You obviously shared something special with them—and they obviously considered you *theirs*."

Rubbing my eyes, I don't point out the irony of how they were jealous of him *first*. Mark's not in any mood to hear it, and quite frankly, I'm just thankful he believes me when only one other person ever listened. Mark's face softens.

"I'm sorry. I'm being rude, demanding things from you

when your plate is already full. Just.... please don't return to Australia. Please, give us a chance."

I suck in a pained breath.

"I can't. Maybe....maybe if you moved to Oz, but I know how unfair it is to ask you to leave your practice behind to live half-way around the world, but I just can't be here. Please understand that."

His honey-hued brown eyes fill with sadness, but he doesn't ask me to stay again.

"Get some rest. I'll see you tomorrow at the memorial service."

Mark leans down to kiss my forehead before walking away, and I don't know what to do but return to my room and lock the door.

How many more times am I going to have to burn my bridges until there's nothing but ash left?

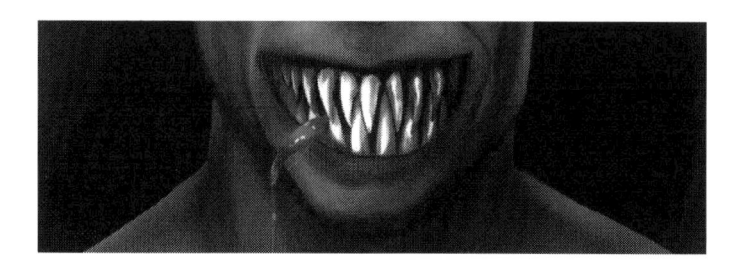

A knock on my room door jars me awake.

"Ms. Stanton?" a booming voice calls.

Warily, I scoot out of bed and crack open the door. In the dimly lit hallway, I see two cops and the elderly B & B owner.

"Yes?" I ask apprehensively.

When the police show up in the dead of the night, it's never a good thing.

"Can you come with us, please? We had a report that someone broke into your house."

Blinking the sleep from my eyes, I nod, asking for a moment while I change. Throwing on a pair of leggings and a hoodie, I grab my purse and join the two men in the hallway.

"Can I trust these men?" I whisper to Mrs. Solday, the B & B owner.

"Of course, dear. They're who they say they are. I'll keep a light on the porch for you, and the front door unlocked."

"Thank you. I apologize—"

"Not your fault," she interrupts. "I just hope everything is alright."

I purse my lips, sighing. Someone breaking into my parents' home is the least of my worries—or cares—but I'm too tired to do anything but follow the cops out to their squad car. I get into the back, like a convicted criminal, and rest my head against the window as we drive to the station. Except, when we stop, we're not at all where I expected to be. We're in front of my house.

At night.

One of the officers steps out of the car and opens the door for me to get out, but I'm rooted to the back seat.

"Ma'am?" he calls, holding out a hand when I don't budge.

All I can do is stare. Every light is blazing inside of the house, but it does nothing to soothe me. In the distance, thunder rumbles, a loud reminder of the storms rolling in. The walkie-talkie attached to the cop's shoulder suddenly chirps, and a garbled voice jumbles out a message that I can't understand. The man before me gives the standard 'ten-four' before reaching inside the vehicle to bodily pull me out.

"They've caught the perpetrator," he announces.

"What?" I gasp, trying to tug free.

"Another unit was already here before we arrived. They've got the man in custody and want to know if you want to press charges."

"Er, nope. It's ok. You caught them—no harm, no foul, right?"

The man looks at me like he wants to argue, but doesn't.

"Very well, please come with me to sign some papers while we escort the trespasser off the property."

The cop walks resolutely toward the house, and I numbly follow. The sooner I sign the release form, the sooner I can go back to bed and forget this night ever happened. In truth, I never planned to come back here. Seeing it now brings a wave of terror and aching pain, reminding me of all that I've lost. Inside, the house is eerily silent; only our footsteps and the thunder can be heard. My breathing escalates into short, desperate pants when the police officer starts trudging up the stairs. As if he can sense my trepidation, he turns to address me.

"Deputy Briggs will have that paper for you to sign; he's waiting upstairs with the culprit."

Rubbing at my chest to ease some of the pressure, I give a silent nod and will my feet to continue forward. Step after step, I climb to the second floor, every inch of my body shaking. To my right is the door to my parents' room, opened wide, but I keep my gaze firmly affixed to the wooden floor, dulled with time. My hand grips the banister tightly like it's my anchor. I bite the inside of my mouth to keep from shattering apart. The taste of blood is a contrast to the whites of my knuckles, which have been leached of the fluid.

"Ma'am?" another cop calls from down the hall.

Slowly, I look up and flinch. He's standing right in front

of my room. The man beckons me to him before turning to walk through the door that leads to my personal hell. Realizing that he's not waiting for me, I force my hand off the stair rail and push onto the landing. The cop who led me upstairs smiles encouragingly. I'm sure he thinks this is difficult because my dad just died. He has no idea of the danger *I'm* in.

Only me because I'm the only one who believes in monsters—*a stipulation for anyone to see them.*

The light is the only thing saving my ass.

Eventually, I make it to my room. Every light is on, including the lamps. It's overkill, but I'm grateful for their luminance. My eyes bounce everywhere, except my bed, and come to rest on the trespasser. A gasp escapes me as my gaze locks with a familiar golden brown one.

"*Mark?!*" I mumble disbelievingly. "What are you doing here?"

Didn't he know how dangerous this place was, whether he believed in monsters or not?

"I was getting a few things for you for tomorrow," he responds tightly.

"What?" I wonder blankly.

Reaching over to my desk, he picks up a box and reaches inside to pull out my mother's jewelry box, a framed photo of my parents, the stuffed bear he got me for my seventeenth birthday, and other various sentimental knickknacks.

"I know you wouldn't come back, but I also know you'd regret selling this place without getting the things that you love. Of course, I'm taking a gander at the majority of the items I collected, but I couldn't let you get on that plane tomorrow without something to remember this place by— to remember me by."

A hiccupping sob fills the air, and I realize it's my own.

The poor cops shuffle from foot to foot, obviously uncomfortable. Stepping toward Deputy Briggs, I ask to sign the release form. Mark offers his sincere apologies, and within minutes, the room clears of the four police officers. I watch as they leave the house and get into their squad cars before disappearing into the night—just in time, too, as the sky lets loose a torrent of rain. I watch the squall for a moment before turning back to Mark.

"You didn't have to do this," I tell him softly.

"I know… it was supposed to be a surprise. I didn't mean for this to happen—for them to bring you *here*. I'm so sorry."

"Well, you can add breaking and entering to your resume, now," I tease with a yawn.

Mark frowns.

"As badass as that sounds, the front door was unlocked. I just waltzed right in."

I bite my lower lip to keep the manic giggle suppressed.

"That's my fault. I was in a rush when I left the other day. I didn't want to linger, and Mrs. Williams was waiting to take Mr. Mittens—"

"You don't have to explain. I have my car out back. Let me give you a lift back to Margie's."

"Thanks, I would appreciate that," I murmur, walking over to peek inside the box he's holding.

My diary's inside, but I take it out.

I don't want to reread the memories written there—besides, they're forever locked in my head, taunting me with the past I can't escape.

Mark doesn't comment when I place the journal on the desk.

"Anything else I should grab?"

Quickly, I rack my brain. The sooner I decide, the sooner I can leave.

"Yes, my dad's lucky fishing lure. It was his grandpa's. Dad kept it on the nightstand beside the bed."

"Ok, let's get it and go," Mark directs.

He tucks the box under an arm and reaches out to hold my hand with the other. I take it, and he squeezes gently, reminding me that I'm not in this alone. Together, we walk out of my room, and Mark deliberately leaves the lights on. Another clap of thunder shakes the house, and I see lightning flash from the windows in my parents' room. Mark walks in to get the fishing lure when I remember Roxy's plaid sweatshirt. For some reason, I can't fathom leaving it behind even though it does nothing but bring back bad memories like my diary.

Quickly wheeling around, I race back to my room, hollering to Mark what I'm doing. Panting, I snatch up the shirt still resting in the far corner of my room. No sooner than I touch the familiar pink fabric, another crash of thunder shatters the night. The wind howls ferociously as the lights in the house flicker once, then twice, before snuffing out. The echoing lightning illuminates the room enough for me to catch my reflection in the mirror hanging on the opposite wall. Pure panic is etched onto my face. The room becomes black as I turn to run, but a hand snakes out to wrap around my ankle. My scream catches in my throat as it yanks me to the ground and under the bed.

Then, everything goes dark.

CHAPTER

TWELVE
Xhoshad

"Where's Seriq?" I wonder, glancing at the limp form of Nerazi.

He's curled into a ball in the corner, his skin a sickly gray. I know if he doesn't get sustenance soon, he'll dissolve back into nothing. His yellow eyes are open, but sightless, their normal vibrant glow dimmed. Nerazi doesn't answer. I'm not entirely sure why I bothered to ask. Sighing, I turn away just as the person in question comes charging through the door with something slung over his shoulder.

Or should I say someone.

Before my disbelieving eyes, Seriq gently lowers a woman I never thought to lay eyes upon again.

Alexis—our human.

Even Nerazi comes to life, lifting his head limply. His dulled eyes drink her in, and I know the minute recognition sparks because his gaze literally flares brightly. In a blur, he shifts into a shadow before resolidifying atop Alexis' body, syphoning the energy from her. I watch the purplish hue of his skin seep back in as our human grows paler.

"Enough!" I roar, darting forward to knock his hulking frame off the smaller one trapped beneath him. "You're killing her!"

Nerazi gives a feral hiss, and attempts to crawl back over, but Seriq steps in front of the unconscious woman, his arms firmly crossed over his chest.

"Mine!" he spits venomously, staring at Nerazi in challenge.

Baring his teeth menacingly at the implacable green-eyed obstruction, Nerazi eases back into the corner shadows. His neon yellow gaze burns angrily at Seriq, but I'm not worried. Nerazi was born of mischief and greed—a relentless combination—but Seriq was born of possessiveness. What he declares as his is *his*. Unfortunately, the human Alexis cannot only belong to him. Seriq will just have to learn to share, which is where I come in.

I was born from coercion, leadership's darker, more sinister sibling.

"Move!" I snap coldly, my tone brooking no argument.

Begrudgingly, Seriq shifts aside while keeping a wary eye on Nerazi. I bend over at the waist and scoop up Alexis into my arms. She looks so small and delicate in comparison to my kind—so breakable. A snarl curls my lips at the thought. No one will harm a hair on her head, or I will tear them apart, piece by excruciatingly painful piece. Turning my back on the others, I stride out of the common room into my private quarters. I gently set the human atop my slumbering pad and undress. My kind doesn't wear clothes and I've longed to see my mate bared before me. I stare hungrily at her a moment before abruptly leaving. Once upon a time, she was a temptation too great to bear, but now, she's grown, here, and *accessible*.

Yet, I'm no monster to use her while she sleeps, no

matter what the humans think of my kind—or did—so very few believe in us anymore.

"How did you find her?" I demand, materializing back in the common room where both Seriq and Nerazi wait, as if frozen.

Seriq's green eyes bore into mine, but no answer tumbles from his lips. Nerazi narrows his own yellow gaze.

"He's been using the portal," he accuses.

I inhale sharply.

"Are you trying to get us dissolved?!"

Seriq growls savagely, shoving past me. I don't bother asking where he's going. Hissing out a sibilant sigh, I acknowledge I should have put Alexis in his room. Anything Seriq deems his eventually ends up there. Briefly, I wonder if I should intervene, but my silent friend has more control than most. He's not formed from impetuousness, as Nerazi, but when you've waited for something this long, restraint doesn't come easily.

"If the false king finds out we have Alexis—"

"I know what will happen," I cut Nerazi off. "That's why we must return her."

It pains me to say it out loud, losing her for a second time is akin to dying slowly, but it's not worth the risk of keeping her here. Nerazi sucks in a shuttering breath before nodding. He knows what I say is true. Now, to convince Seriq.

"No!" a voice shouts behind me. I turn to see the green-eyed giant stalking toward me. "Mine! Mine! Mine!"

Seriq repeats this singular word of ownership as he lowers his head and charges me. I tense a mere second before his solid form crashes into mine. Sharp teeth come dangerously close to my face before I shift into shadow form and reappear on the other side of the room. Rolling my shoulders, my muscles bunch together in anticipation.

If Seriq wants a fight, he's got one.

Raising my claws, I leap from the corner, launching myself high into the air. Seriq meets me half-way, never one to shy away from a confrontation. Instead of explosive words, he battles with barely compressed violence. I know he would never kill me, but Seriq doesn't hold back when we brawl like this. If I don't keep my wits about me, I'll end up severely maimed—again.

We collide midair, dropping down to the ground. The heavy weight of our fall echoes like the thunder heard in the human world. Briefly, I worry about us waking Alexis, but Nerazi deeply depleted her. Only many hours of rest will restore her to a semblance of health again. Sharp claws rake across my back and right arm, forcing a pained growl from my lips. Kicking out heavily, I wrap a phantom hand around both of Seriq's ankles and pull, yanking him onto his back.

In answer, he wraps a shadow arm around my waist, effectively holding me at bay as we swipe viciously at one another. Surprisingly, it's Nerazi who separates us. Seriq and I are so focused on one another that neither of us see him disappear. In seconds, he reappears between us, shoving our forms in opposite directions. His yellow eyes glow with malice, and they're leveled on me.

"We're keeping her," he snarls.

My face lifts in puzzlement. Nerazi never sides with Seriq—*ever*—possession and greed rarely get along. Running a taloned hand over my smooth head, I scowl crossly, weighing my options. Seriq is a formidable opponent that I've only beaten a handful of times over the millennia of our existence. Logically, there's no way I'll win against *both* of them, but the consequences of keeping

Alexis here are dire enough I must try. Cracking my neck to the side, I curl a claw in invitation at Nerazi and Seriq. The latter stares silently—resolutely—but Nerazi laughs in disbelief.

"You're going to die," he declares, stating the obvious.

I grunt in answer. If I meet my demise, at least I know I tried to protect the human—and ourselves. Both Seriq and Nerazi lower into a crouch; I mirror their movements, hoping my plan of attack is one step ahead of theirs. Just as I'm about to spring into action, a sound catches my attention. As one, the three of us turn to see a pale, shaky Alexis. She's on all fours, crawling around like an animal.

"What are you doing?" I wonder out loud to her, the sounds of her language garbled in my mouth.

Halting, a look of panic rolls across her face. Biting her lip—a trait I forgot she does when nervous—Alexis slowly inches forward, uncertainty stamped into her lovely features.

"I can't see," she admits in a husky voice that frazzles my mind. "I can only... *perceive* things."

Her face scrunches up at this as she squints. The darkness of our land is easily pierced by the brightness of our eyes, but for humans, it takes them years to adapt and see as well as we do. I look blankly at Seriq and Nerazi, not entirely understanding what Alexis said.

"What do you mean?" I prompt, wondering if I misinterpreted her words.

It's been a long time since I've heard and spoken her human tongue.

"I don't know how to explain it. The only thing I can see is your eyes," she flinches, "everything else is like a shadowed blob that I'm guessing what it is. Am... am I going blind?"

"No!" I rush to explain. "Our world is a murky one—your eyes merely need to adapt to the lack of light."

Alexis shudders, wrapping an arm around her waist, her face forlorn and sickly.

"I want to go home."

Her words slice through me, more piercing than any talon, and tear through my bloodlust. Deep down, I crave an indescribable harmony so elusive to my kind that Alexis represents—

Peace.

Hope.

Love.

The opposite emotions from which my kind is born, and therefore, cannot fathom. To keep her is selfish and dangerous. For the first time in my existence, I'm trying to be altruistic, but that doesn't mean I'm happy about my internal decision. Nor do I delight in Alexis' wish to go home. If times were different, she wouldn't have a say. I'd chain her to my slumbering quarters to use for my pleasure.

"She wants to go home," I murmur sadly in my language to Seriq and Nerazi.

"She can't," Nerazi refutes. "We need her—*I* need her."

His voice cracks in a way that makes me question if this is more than just his greed to have her.

"We'll find another," I counter, making Seriq snort.

"No," he barks without elaborating.

"Our time is dwindling, the portals are shrinking, and another woman will *never* do," Nerazi reminds hotly.

Groaning, I know he's right. To return her means death for the rest of us—but to keep her means death for *all* of us. Surely the others don't want that fate for Alexis, but Nerazi's face reflects a confidence I don't feel. He thinks we can outrun those who will hunt us down, but I have my doubts. The yellow-eyed fiend clicks his long tongue.

"Since when do you give up?"

I glare at the insinuation.

"This isn't about "giving up", it's about doing what's right—"

"Wrong!" Seriq snaps, taking me aback.

Nerazi smirks, and I realize my logic is wasted.

"What are you saying?" Alexis suddenly inquires, attempting to stand.

She wobbles a bit, and I reach out a hand to brace her on her feet.

"You need to rest," I hedge in response.

"No," she bites out defiantly, making Seriq hiss. "Tell me or take me home."

Her response makes my blood heat, and I hear Nerazi mumble, "She's grown impudent."

In our world, impudence is met with punishment, and I grow hard at the thought of punishing her soft flesh.

"Ours," Seriq suddenly spits.

I give him a questioning look, but Nerazi nods.

"Alexis is ours. We can't let her go."

Heaving a weary sigh, I know they're right. We *should* return her to the human world, but it's not what I want to do—what any of us want to do.

"She will fight us," I protest weakly.

Seriq bares his teeth in an animalistic leer that Nerazi copies.

"We look forward to it," he purrs.

I glance at Alexis, who is nibbling her lip apprehensively. The soft pink of her race is slowly returning to her cheeks, gracing her with vitality and allure once more.

"We'll have to run," I warn the others. "We'll never be safe."

They nod in acknowledgement.

"Fine," I finally concede, "we'll keep her, but first things first—she must be marked."

Seriq tips back his head and howls in victory, the eerie sound causing Alexis to jump. She has no idea what we've decided, but is intuitive enough to realize it's not in her favor. She turns to dash away, and a triumphant smile twists my lips. She just gave us the very thing we desire—*to chase her*. She can run but there's nowhere to hide, and when we catch her...

I'll make her submit to me.

THIRTEEN
Alexis

I realize too late my mistake the instant the lights go out and something wraps around my ankle. Pain explodes in my head as it smacks the carpeted floor of my old bedroom hard, then my world goes dark—but whether it's because I pass out or something else, I don't know. What I do know is that I'm not in Texas anymore.

My head throbs intensely when my eyes flutter open. I can't make out much in the dark, shadowed room, but I recognize enough to know I've never been here before. As I will my eyes to see, a terrible hissing reaches my ears first. It gets louder and louder, a terrifying sound that's also familiar—something I've heard in my dreams.

Or nightmares.

Gasping, I sit up and promptly fall back again on a soft pad of fabric. I feel so weak and depleted. Carefully reaching out with my hands, I blindly search my surroundings. Whatever I'm perched on isn't very high off the ground. I slide off and crawl toward the sibilant voices, discerning at least two. I can't understand what's being said, but I know who's talking—just like I knew that one day, they would take me.

But *where* is the question.

Arduously, I make my way to a room no less dim than the hall I just crawled through. I pause in the archway, taking in three sets of glowing eyes I haven't seen in twelve years—except in my nightmares. I blink rapidly to bring the scene into focus, but everything remains hazy and blurred. The panic I felt before doubles in horror when my eyes can't make out anything but their eyes. The familiar scarlet gaze of Xhoshad turns on me as he speaks in the hissing sound earlier before addressing me in English.

I realize what I thought was a den of snakes talking is really their language.

"What are you doing?" Xhoshad demands in a harsh voice, made even coarser by the difficult vowels and consonants of my tongue.

Trying not to cry, I murmur, "I can't see. I can only *perceive* things."

Xhoshad glances back at Nerazi and Seriq, telling them something I can't understand. After a moment, he asks me to elaborate.

"I don't know how to explain it. The only thing I can see are your eyes. Everything else is like a shadowed blob. Am I going blind?"

My voice trembles, revealing the depth of my fear.

"No! Our world is a murky one—your eyes merely need to adapt to the lack of light," the shadowy monster calms.

Wrapping my arm around my waist, I lean back to sit, pulling my knees to my chest. I feel sick to my stomach and scared.

How can I make any decisions if I can't even see?

"I want to go home," I whisper more to myself than to them.

There's a beat of silence before Xhoshad starts hissing at Nerazi and Seriq. The yellow-eyed monster seemingly continues his argument from before while the green-eyed one offers only a single word in comment. Apparently, he speaks little in general. The thought makes me uneasy.

The quiet ones are always the instigators.

Although I can't say for certain, it feels like Xhoshad is championing my cause, but after a minute, I don't hear the same conviction in his voice. Whatever he's saying, he's wavering. Then, Seriq tips his head back to blend completely into the darkness and howls into the black. The sound stops my heart, and I slam forward, returning to all fours. Unconsciously, I turn and scramble back toward where I came. Realistically, I know it won't do me any good. There aren't even any doors, and I'm basically blind, but the instinct to run is reflexive—*that's what a normal person does when confronted with feral monsters.*

Crawling back into the room I originally was in, I toss a glance over my shoulder, but no glowing eyes follow me and silence greets me. Maybe I misinterpreted their hisses, and they are giving me space. Except, I forget that my monsters are one with the shadows, silent and stealthy. No sooner than I hit the soft pad on the floor, the inky silhouettes of the three monsters descend upon me, voracious and hungry. At first, they are just wisps, but slowly, they solidify into their solid forms. Xhoshad is in front of me; Seriq is watching from a short distance, meaning the weight at my back must be Nerazi.

"Comfortable?" he croons sweetly.

Too sweetly.

Although depleted, I tip my head back to glare at him,

remembering his tendency to put on a charming front. He chuckles darkly, as if amused.

"Such impudence," Nerazi declares with relish. "Our Alexis has fire."

"Firstly, I'm not "your" anything," I spit venomously. "Secondly, we have a saying in English—play with fire; get burned."

"Mmmmm," the bastard hums. "You were right, Xhoshad; she is going to fight us."

"She can try," the red-eyed monster responds genially, inching forward while parting my legs.

My traitorous body arches unintentionally into his touch, my knees widening to accommodate his large, muscled body. Every neuron in my body is firing, every nerve ending snapping to attention. I've never felt so alive, but at the same time, my brain is short-circuiting, unsure how to proceed.

"You can't have sex with me—not without my permission," I snarl.

Nerazi laughs again, making my blood boil.

"We don't plan to "have sex with you"; we're going to mark you and—"

"*Fuck you*," Seriq finishes in a guttural tone, and I wonder where he learned the word.

"M-m-mark me?" I quiver.

"Yesssss," Xhoshad hisses, his face so close to mine that I can make out his gleaming, pointed teeth twisted into a smile. "Mark you—*claim you*—and we don't need *your* permission. Your body already has given it."

I gasp at his audacity.

"I beg your fucking—"

"Hear that, brothers, she's begging to be fucked," Nerazi taunts, and I struggle vainly against his hold.

"Argh!" I scream, pissed beyond measure. "I wasn't begging you to fuck me!"

"Liar," Seriq's voice drifts over to me.

I glare at the green-eyed monster watching everything unfold daring him to say, but of course, he doesn't.

"I'm not ly—"

"We can *smell* you," Xhoshad growls. "Your lust, your need."

"Your *pussy*," Seriq adds, making me squirm.

"Lie to yourself all you want," Nerazi purrs into my ear from behind me, "but your body can't deceive us. You might say no, but we know you really mean yes."

I don't answer, too embarrassed to say anything because —*they're right*. Intellectually, I'm fighting, but physically, my body is one hundred percent on board. *And always has been.* If I'm being truthful with myself, I've always feared my reaction to them, the intense desire they stir within my center. Even now, weak and unseeing, I'm dripping wet.

"I don't belong here!" I argue, not having the faintest idea where 'here' even is, but Xhoshad puts a finger to my lips.

"This is where you've belonged all along," he counters gravely.

"And that is...."

"Spread before us, ours for the taking."

Before I can snap something pithy, his long, wet tongue snakes out to lick lightly down the inside of my thigh. I gasp in shock at the sensation, the cool air leaving a trail of goosebumps wherever his tongue touches. Behind me, Nerazi mimics Xhoshad, licking first my neck, but then stretching forward to curl his tongue around my right breast. The tip flicks the nipple, and I can feel the serpentine split at the end. Against my will, I moan.

"Still want to tell us you don't want this?" Nerazi challenges just as Xhoshad's tongue flicks across the apex of my legs.

The red-eyed monster hasn't moved, demonstrating how very long his tongue is, indeed. I scowl into the dark, not bothering to answer Nerazi, but the trouble-maker persists in tormenting me.

"I'm so sorry you can't see," he continues in faux kindness. "Let me tell you what Seriq's doing."

I buck back, hoping to stall his words, but Nerazi just sweeps an arm around my torso, locking me tightly against him. Unable to move, Xhoshad spreads my thighs wider, his tongue delving into the wetness between them. I cry out at the sensation of his forked tongue laving my clit roughly.

"His tongue is wrapped around his cock," Nerazi whispers, painting a lurid and provocative scene in my head. "Slowly, up and down, he licks his cock, just like Xhoshad licks *you*."

"Uhhhh," I pant, unable to erase the image from my mind.

I imagine Seriq climaxing just as Xhoshad pushes deeply into my pussy—*and I explode.* My keening cry of pleasure echoes around the cavernous room, but quickly turns to one of surprise mixed with pain as Xhoshad reaches forward to rake his nails lightly across the plains of my flat stomach. The metallic tang of my blood fills the air, so strong that I can almost taste it. Tears dot my eyes, not understanding at all what just happened.

"Why did you—" I attempt, but Nerazi is pushing me forward.

"My turn," he rumbles in his deep, accented voice.

I land sprawled on my injured stomach, my face against

Xhoshad's bulging cock. From behind, I can feel Nerazi licking the globe of my right cheek.

"No!" I cry, alarmed at the emotions bombarding my body at his actions. "Not there.... it's *private*."

"No part of you is private," the cocksure monster announces. "When we're done, we'll own *every* inch of you."

My body trembles at his words knowing he means every single one of them, but to my surprise, the yellow-eyed menace doesn't do at all what I expected. Instead of his tongue doing unspeakable things to my ass, a clawed finger dips into my pussy. Instinctively, I clench in trepidation, fear heightening everything inside of me. I breathe shallowly as he starts to finger fuck me, praying he doesn't cut me instead. But Nerazi has perfect control of his deadly nail, it seems, the sharp point barely kissing the corners of my warmth. The quick scratch of agony is chased by the intense pleasure that follows; back and forth this continues until I once more reach a peak. I crash over the edge, coming hard, when Nerazi uses his other hand to score my lower back much as Xhoshad did my stomach.

Instead of stunting my orgasm, it only deepens it.

"What the fuck!" I howl in confusion and ecstasy.

"*My* turn," a husky voice sighs.

I feel both Xhoshad and Nerazi pull away from me as Seriq steps into my space. His neon green eyes dominate my vision, and I yearn to see more, but secretly enjoy the helpless feeling of not knowing what's going to happen. It's like being blindfolded. Seriq's enormous hand reaches out to encircle my neck, reminding me of how easily any one of them could kill me. But these monsters don't want to slaughter me—*they want to dominate me.* Seriq demonstrates this by shoving his dick into my mouth.

Unlike the others who controlled me through my pleasure, Seriq commands me through *his*. Initially, I gag at the large and unexpected intrusion, but relax into the green-eyed monster's touch. I gasp in surprise when I feel his tongue touch mine—like a French kiss while we both lick his cock at the same time. Impulsively, I wrap my hands around his length, stroking him in tandem to the movements of our tongues dueling across his pulsing flesh.

I work him harder and faster, circulating my mouth around his engorged head—my lips stretched as far as they can go—when Seriq squeezes my throat firmly. To my surprise, my lips spread even wider as he pushes into me in a punishing manner. A growling hiss is the only warning I get that he's about to come before a deluge of monster cream coats both of our tongues. The flavor is unlike anything I've ever experienced before and more akin to something I've smelled.

Like the crispness of the night air mixed with spices.

Moaning at the taste, I lap it up greedily, swallowing it down like it's my last meal. In response, my body seems to come alive again. The fatigued enervation I previously felt transforms into resurgence. I blink as my eyes become more focused, allowing me to pierce the darkness just a bit. Seriq's body is outlined before me, and I can almost see the deep purple tone of his skin. His long tongue is wrapped three times around his massive cock, which is still dripping cum.

Without thinking, I lean forward to catch the bright lime-colored drops of his otherworldly seed. Seriq bares his teeth at the motion, swiping out with a black-tipped talon, raking it from the bottom of my left ear to the top of my right breast. Shrieking in distress from the disconcerting sting, I lash out to push the monstrous man away. More blood drips from this new wound as tears well up in my eyes.

"Why are you hurting me?" I sniffle, feeling betrayed.

Xhoshad pushes Seriq aside.

"We're marking you," he explains, making me furious.

"I don't know what that means!"

"It means you're ours—forever," Nerazi adds from somewhere in the room. "Marking wounds heal quickly, leaving only a scar."

Frowning, I reach down to where Xhoshad first clawed my stomach. Sure enough, the open wound is gone, but it's still too dark for me to see the white traces of a scar. Twisting a hand behind my back, Nerazi's mark is already healed. Startled, I clamp a hand to my throat, which still feels raw, but the skin is already stitching itself back together.

"I don't understand—"

"Breeding marks tell all other Vasura that you've been claimed—*by us*. No one else can fuck you, touch you, even look at you."

"You're mine," Seriq affirms.

"*Ours*," Nerazi corrects sternly, but Seriq merely shrugs.

I toss my hands up in irritation, not even wanting to have this argument again.

"Listen, I'm not yours—no matter what my body "says" —you still need my permission. Besides, I already, er, *belong* to someone—and I use the word loosely," I lie.

"The human!" Seriq spits vituperatively.

I freeze, unsure how to proceed. Xhoshad stares at me with his blood-red eyes, leveling me with a glare.

"We will kill him," he declares, my throat convulsing at the promise.

"No! I-I didn't mean it!"

Seriq hisses something in his tongue that has the others

responding heatedly, and I long to speak their language as they do mine.

"What are you saying?" I wonder, tugging on Xhoshad's arm to get his attention, but a loud banging noise erupts somewhere not too far away.

Nerazi curses savagely in English, jarring me off the soft fabric pad.

"What's wrong?" I whisper.

"It's the Revenant Swarm," he answers in a rush. "Seriq, quick, take her and run! Xhoshad and I will detain them."

The green-eyed monster wastes no time scooping me up and fading into black smoke. Although in his shadow form, his touch is still tangible against my very bare skin. We shoot out a window into the chilly darkness and into the blackened sky. I can't tell if it's night or day, but below us, a large cave system dances into sight before the dimness swallows it. Higher and higher we fly, and I'm too discombobulated to be afraid.

"Where are we going?"

I shiver from the cool air against my exposed skin. Seriq doesn't answer, and I gnash my teeth together in annoyance. Of course, Nerazi told him to come with me. He doesn't talk —and therefore, won't tell me a damn thing!

Who is the Revenant Swarm?
Why are they attacking?
Will Xhoshad and Nerazi be ok?

Huffing, I start to question Seriq again, but he presses a wisp of a finger to my lips.

"Hush—you're safe," he soothes, tracing the finger against the mark he slashed into my neck.

I open my mouth to argue, but a sweeping lethargy drifts over me, making my eyelids heavy. Although I don't know how, I'm sure it's Seriq, using some monstrous form of compulsion over me.

"We're not done talking," I murmur sleepily.

Seriq's chuckle is the last thing I hear before the shadows gobble me up.

CHAPTER FOURTEEN
Nerazi

My body buzzes with power—*both from Alexis' arousal and from marking her.* Normally, it would take much more to restore me, but the combination of the two has catapulted me into a new echelon of strength. The Fallacious will regret hunting us this day. Next to me, Xhoshad widens his stance, bending at the knees while extending his claws. It's a trait of my kind to be able to retract or grow them at will.

The barrier breaks down and shadows blast into the room, solidifying into one monstrous entity. Xhoshad shifts, the only sign of his apprehension. The Revenant Swarm is dangerous because The Fallacious' army is built of thousands of wraiths who used to be whole, but have succumbed to the emotion that created them. Without a mate, my kind ceases to exist—unless another, more powerful Vasura harnesses the base emotion at the core of them.

Like The Fallacious has done with these men.

I suppress a shudder, wondering how close I had been to dissolving into nothing. Before Alexis showed up, I hadn't fed in so long. Every day, I grew fainter and fainter, but I knew Xhoshad and Seriq wouldn't let our corrupt leader get to me. If I had become nothing more than my base emotion, I would have been a specter of greed—a very dangerous weapon for The Fallacious to wield.

It makes me wonder what deadly emotions are at the core of the lumbering monster before me.

From the corner of my eye, two more pairs of shadow arms push out of Xhoshad's side. He's trying to even the playing field, and I follow suit—I just hope our twelve hands are enough to get us out of here alive. The Revenant Swarm wastes no time, lashing out with decisive intent. Xhoshad jumps up and over it, raking his claws into its side while I dip low and do the same to the creature's leg.

The Revenant Swarm bursts into hundreds of wisps before reforming a small distance behind Xhoshad and me. A knowing glint shimmers in its eyes, and I don't doubt one of its base emotions is cunning. I bare my teeth in challenge, welcoming its skill. If it had come only hours before, I might have joined its cause—*I had so very little to live for*—but Seriq changed that when he took Alexis. Now, I feel invincible. The Revenant Swarm is made of many devious emotions, but I'm composed of voracity.

Insatiability is an unbeatable trait—I'll keep coming for more until there's nothing left.

Diving forward in a swooping motion, the creature unfurls its tongue to wrap around Xhoshad's six arms, lifting him high into the air. He roars furiously as the Revenant Swarm brings him toward its sharp teeth, intent on eating one I consider my brother. Pushing my claws even longer until they merge into a single, lethal talon, I run toward the wall behind the monster. Exploding into shadow form, I fly up toward the high ceiling of our home structure, tucking into myself to backflip off of the Revenant Swarm's exposed tongue.

Using my combined nail like a scythe, I sever the spongey, red flesh binding Xhoshad. The Revenant Swarm screeches in fury and pain as its tongue drops to the ground and shatters into individual Vasura. They lay there, gray and sickly, much as I did not too long before. Without The Fallacious to reharness their base emotion, my brethren will cease to exist. I feel a moment of sadness at their fate, wasting away into nothing, but the Revenant Swarm is oblivious. Xhoshad is back on his feet, but looks shaken as he takes in the dying Vasura.

"Did I look this bad?" I bite out jokingly.

"Worse," he attests seriously, and I know I owe Seriq my life.

Bowing my head, I prepare to strike out against the Revenant Swarm once more, but the creature doesn't attack. Instead, it watches, as if calculating a plan. Then, it disbands into its individual shadows, shrieking like the wind out the door and into the dark.

"What the fuck just happened?" Xhoshad snarls.

I snick my teeth together in contemplation.

"That thing is shrewd. Whatever base emotions The Fallacious harnessed for this particular army, intelligence was its mission."

Xhoshad ponders my words for a moment.

"A spying Revenant Swarm...." he postulates, waving away his extra shadow limbs. "Then we are in more trouble than I previously thought. If that thing's only purpose was to gather information and take it back to our leader, then—"

"It knows about Alexis," I finish.

"We must breed her. The sooner she is fecund, the safer she'll be."

Snorting, I become one with the night, soaring out of the caves we called home and into the sky above. Xhoshad follows me, keeping an eye out for anyone who might be trailing us.

"She'll never be safe," I point out after we are a secure distance away.

Xhoshad's red eyes narrow in menace as he glares at me.

"I know," he snarls. "That's why I didn't want to keep her!"

"That wasn't an option, either," I counter, lapsing into silence. Sighing, I ask, "How long has Seriq been using the portal?"

Shrugging, Xhoshad answers, "Not a fucking clue. Long enough to alert the Revenant Swarm."

Our eyes lock, both reflecting the same fear for Alexis and one another. If The Fallacious finds out about her, he'll stop at nothing to take her from us.

"You don't think...." I trail off, and Xhoshad shakes his head.

"He doesn't know about Alexis, or his army wouldn't have stopped—"

"Then why—"

"I don't know," Xhoshad murmurs. "It doesn't make any sense. If The Fallacious knew Seriq was using the portal, why didn't he send his Revenant Swarm to punish us accordingly?" *The punishment being death.* "What was he scouting for?"

The question disturbs me.

"Not our mate," I conclude.

Normally, a Vasura can easily scent a human woman, but when my kind succumbs to nothing and another harnesses their base emotion, they are little more than just that feeling. They might operate like they're still alive but essentially are dead. Knowing this, the Vasura within The Fallacious' Revenant Swarm couldn't have smelled Alexis. Perhaps they saw Seriq with her on his way to our caves, but it doesn't explain why Fallacious sent reconnaissance. Xhoshad flies silently beside me, pondering my words.

"I don't like this new development. We must join Seriq and Alexis immediately," he concludes.

"And do what? Go where?" I demand.

There isn't any place that The Fallacious doesn't taint, except the human world, but we can't survive there. There's too much light, especially now with modern technology. Humans don't sleep anymore. They aren't afraid anymore. They don't believe in us anymore, and now my kind is wasting away into nothingness because of it.

"The Bowels," Xhoshad whispers.

"What?" I cringe, hoping I heard him wrong.

"We go to The Bowels."

"Are you fucking crazy? There's no way we can take Alexis down there."

The Bowels is an underground cave system filled with terrifying beasts that make my kind seem friendly. It's where unlawful Vasura are banished and is basically a death sentence.

"I know someone who can help us," Xhoshad insists.

Clicking my teeth together, I give no reply, wondering who he could possibly know that survived and is living in The Bowels. Over the centuries, I've learned that Xhoshad is resourceful and cunning—*key elements for him to effectively manipulate his base emotion of coercion*. I wait for him to explain more—or perhaps even force me—but the red-eyed Vasura remains silent, lost in his own thoughts.

I follow his lead, although I can smell Seriq's and Alexis' trail well enough. The three of us marked one another to form a trium, a pod of Vasura with a single mate, when we found Alexis all those years ago. Even then, we knew she would be ours. Marking a fellow Vasura is nothing like marking a mate. There's only pain, but the promise of brotherhood. It's what allows Xhoshad and I to track Seriq, as well as Alexis.

My mind wanders to the beautiful, four-fingered scratches on her back. Her pain mixed with pleasure was the most potent flavor, one I hope to savor again and again in the future. Even if The Fallacious finds Alexis, she's been claimed three times over. There is no denying to whom she belongs. The thought makes me hard, even in shadow form the blood rushes to my cock, springing it to life.

"Focus," Xhoshad snaps, smelling my arousal more than seeing it.

"I am!" I retort, earning me a glare.

"Don't lie to me. I know you're thinking about her—I am, too, but we have to be careful. Who knows where The Fallacious is lurking—the false king has eyes everywhere."

The thought makes me uneasy.

"Where is Seriq going?" I wonder.

"To The Malevolands. Our ruler usually doesn't go there since it borders The Bowels."

I scowl, not liking the thought. The Malevolands are just as dangerous as the other place, but Seriq has the right idea—that area is bad, but The Fallacious is *worse*. As long as the Revenant Swarm didn't follow us, they won't know where we've gone. Sight is the only sense they can use, but sparingly. Xhoshad and I continue to soar, one with the smokey darkness surrounding us, until we cross over into The Malevolands. I can feel the change in temperature even in shadow form. The icy air suddenly becomes warmer, a sign that The Bowels are nearby. The caverns are warmed by the underground volcanoes that formed them.

Closing my eyes, I focus on my bond with Seriq and Alexis. Like an invisible beacon, it directs me a short distance to a grove of odollam trees. The barb-tipped leaves are poisonous, but can't pierce us in our shadow-form, making it a safe place to hide for the time being. Only another Vasura could ambush us—*and my kind doesn't visit The Malevolands*. I glide through the foliage to find an amusing scene. Alexis is stomping about, ranting, while Seriq is doing his best to ensure no leaves touch our mate's delicate skin.

"Watch out," I warn smugly, "the tree is fatal."

She freezes mid-tirade, narrowing her eyes in speculation as if deciding whether to believe me or not. I smile, showing off my razor-sharp teeth in a mocking smirk meant to stoke her ire. It succeeds, and I can practically see the steam spouting out her ears.

"That's not funny!" she admonishes, but Xhoshad lifts a hand to silence her.

"It wasn't a joke. Odollam tree leaves are poisonous—even to Vasura."

"Vasura"

"I believe humans call us 'bogeymen'," I supply.

Alexis makes a humming sound that sends the blood rushing back to my cock. It doesn't help that she's nude still, something we'll have to remedy. Even though The Bowels are warm, she's used to wearing clothes, unlike my kind. Clothing is a human thing; the only one who bothers to don them is The Fallacious. The false king thinks that by putting on the ceremonial robes of tribal chieftains, it makes him a god.

In reality, he's nothing but a monstrous liar.

"Why didn't Seriq say something about the leaves?" Alexis bursts out.

I toss back my head and laugh, earning another fierce glare from my mate.

"How could he have told you—you probably haven't been quiet long enough for him to do so," I tease.

She steps up to me, jabbing a finger into me, her bright, blue eyes flashing. Already, they have the faintest glow of one adapting to our darkness. Her smell permeates my senses, sending me into hyper-arousal.

"Don't think I don't know why you sent him with me," she smarts as her unruly blond hair curls into her face.

She pushes at it absentmindedly, and I tug at one upturned end. The length is a few inches longer than it was all those years ago, and I feel a sadness at the thought of young Alexis.

"Where did you go?" I murmur, not realizing I spoke out loud.

Xhoshad hisses at me in our language, and I promptly clamp my mouth shut, but the woman before me isn't letting this go. Her eyes widen at my words, another tempest brewing in their depths.

"You have the audacity to ask me where I went?! YOU STOLE MY BEST FRIEND!"

"By accident," Seriq adds unhelpfully.

"BY ACCIDENT?!" she roars, but Xhoshad shushes her.

"Here is not the place. We will answer your questions—and you will answer ours," he counters, "but first, we must get somewhere safe."

Alexis starts shaking her head, but I step forward, taking her small hand in my much larger one. The contrast between the two is truly night and day. Her skin is a pale, whitish color; whereas mine is a dark purplish-gray. Her nails are small, squared, and colored with the same sparkly substance that she put on them in her youth. Mine are black, sharp, and deadly. My palm easily triples her's in size, engulfing her hand as I stare into her eyes.

"Trust us," I insist.

Alexis gives me a wary look, and I know I'm the last person that should be requesting this of her. I'm a trickster, bent on devilry, but everything hinges on her ability to cede control to us. She's blinded and vulnerable in this land and needs us to protect her. Of course, I could explain this to her, more easily gaining her trust, but the asshole in me enjoys pushing her to her limits. I'm the one in charge and demand that she submit to me.

"I don't know if I can trust you...." Alexis admits, earning an angry hiss from Seriq.

"Please," I bite out despite myself.

Alexis looks down at our entwined hands, sucking in on her bottom lip.

"For now," she grants, looking into all our eyes.

I frown, but don't push the issue. For now will have to do....

Until we can change it to forever.

FIFTEEN
Alexis

Trust them?

The idea is as foreign to me as the land I've been dropped in. I haven't trusted anyone in years, even myself—*especially* myself. Obviously, I'm a terrible judge in character. My lack of faith in anyone has shaped my life into a lonely one, but I realize that right now, I have little choice but to trust these monsters.

Especially after they marked me—whatever that fully means.

But Xhoshad promised to answer my questions; I hope he's ready for all the millions I have. The only thing more numerous than my questions is the emotions overwhelming my brain. Shock, worry, anger, lust, anxiety, fear, and a hint of joy are all bound together in a tangled ball at the pit of my stomach. Worry and anxiety take the forefront, a mirror of my kidnappers' emotions.

What do monsters fear?

Whatever it is can't be good.

Lust comes in second, the feeling both angering me and

unnerving me. Now isn't the time to be craving their monstrous touch, not after everything that's transpired, but I've come to the inevitable conclusion that I don't control my body.

They do.

"Where are my clothes?" I ask quietly, unsure of how much danger we're all in.

Xhoshad grumbles something under his breath, and I squint to bring him more into focus. Everything is still mostly a shadowy blob, but their glowing eyes help me make out their faces and, to an extent, their bodies.

"What? I couldn't hear you."

"He tore them off of you—you know, before when we were—"

"I remember," I cut off Nerazi, turning to glare at Xhoshad.

"What am I going to wear now?"

"Nothing," Seriq purrs in satisfaction.

Nerazi nods in agreement, the smartass.

"I can't just be naked," I splutter.

"Why not?" he counters. "We are."

My prudish gasp is muffled by the odollam tree.

They were naked?

How come I never noticed?

The lust I feel quickly takes center place as I try to discern more through the murkiness that seems to permeate this world.

"We will get you some clothes," Xhoshad reassures. "I know a place that should have some."

Nerazi fires something at him in their language. The red-eyed monster hisses a reply, and I'm left wondering what they're saying. Xhoshad nods at Seriq, who transforms into a wisp before scooping me up like before. He takes off, through the leaves that hang like a willow tree, and I cower in his embrace knowing that they are deadly.

"How come they don't hurt you—or me?" I call out, knowing Seriq won't answer me.

"They can't pierce our shadow forms. As long as Seriq has you covered, you're safe," Xhoshad surprises me by answering, and I relax a bit.

"Can you please tell me where we're going, or what's happening?"

"Soon," he swears. "We must be alert as we travel through the Malevolands into The Bowels."

"The Bowels?" I echo in alarm. "Where are we—*a shitter in Hell?!*"

Nerazi snorts on a laugh. Of course, he would find my sarcasm amusing.

"Just be patient," the yellow-eyed instigator commands, and I fight the urge to scream, squirming in Seriq's arms.

"Be still," he directs in a firm whisper.

I feel my eyes twitch at the overload of bossiness. Looking back on it, they'd always been this way, but in the confines of my bedroom, their domineering ways weren't so prodigious. It was in little, simple things that they demonstrated their control.

A hand around my ankle.

Shadows boxing me in.

Small orders—tell me about your day, how are you feeling, etc.—that were genuine, but also for their benefit.

Back then, I needed that dominance. It gave me structure that I lacked in my day-to-day life with my parents. I craved it, even, but now I'm grown. I don't need be to placated or treated like a child, nor am I too stupid to comprehend I know nothing about the situation that we're in—*that they put me in*—but it could be explained. They could treat me like an equal. Instead, they're treating me like a—

"*Queen.* You're our queen," Seriq whispers in a quiet hiss into my ear, his long, forked tongue tickling the outer shell near my earring.

I still in his smoky arms, not daring to move.

Can he....*read my mind?!*

Nerazi looks over at me, a wicked grin painting his lips; he winks before shooting ahead.

Fuck.

Xhoshad swoops over, his glowing crimson eyes the only indication he's still there amidst the wispiness of his shadow form.

"What's wrong?" he queries, and I roll my eyes.

"Can't you just read my mind—or can only Seriq do that?"

Both monsters chuckle.

"We can't read your mind," Xhoshad assures, "but we can taste your emotions. It's easy to know what you're feeling."

"Taste? Like eat?"

"Not in the human sense, but yes. We can sense your vexation at us—and see it," he laughs again. "Your face is a mirror to your inner thoughts, but please trust us enough to get you to safety first before we explain anything."

I mull over his words before snuggling deeper into Seriq's arms.

"How long before we get to safety?"

Xhoshad takes a moment to respond, and I wonder if he's calculating or debating.

"Maybe twenty human minutes," is his answer.

Peering over Seriq's form, I stare into the dark abyss

below. Of course, I can't see a thing, which only adds to my frustration.

"Is it always this dark?" I lament, mostly to myself.

"Yesssss," Seriq hisses, and I surrender to the truth that I might never know what's happening in this world around me.

I'm completely at these monsters' mercy.

My heart gallops at the thought, unsure if I'm intrigued or alarmed by the idea. The temperature suddenly spikes around us—not just because of my thoughts—and I'm marginally glad to be naked. Sweat drips down the side of my face, falling into the black below me. Occasionally, I hear a sizzle or a crackle echo off in the distance, followed by strange grunts.

What other monsters lurk in the opaque, hazy depths?

It's hard to imagine other creatures more frightening than my Bogeymen, but I realize that their world might contain beasts a thousand times scarier—a very unsettling thought. The external warmth continues to escalate until I feel like I'm being cooked alive. The three monsters seem impervious, and I wonder if their shadow forms even register the jump in temperature.

"It's hot," I pant, the humidity almost suffocating.

"It's the volcanoes," Nerazi's voice drifts back to me. "There's a chain of them underground. The steam escapes through vents below us."

My mind brings up an image I saw once in a TV documentary about the ocean. Towering spires that spit out scorching condensation into the surrounding watery bottoms. Is that what the Malevolands look like? I try to paint a mental picture of the scenery, but my canvas remains blank—or should I say 'black'. I never realized how much I rely on my sense of sight until this moment. Not seeing is not knowing.

And not knowing can be deadly.

"Trust us," Seriq reminds, once more making me question whether he can read minds.

Xhoshad said they can 'taste' my feelings, but are they so strong to give clarity to my thoughts? Or is Seriq divining them another way? I wonder if the marks the three monsters etched into my body have anything to do with it.

"We're almost there," Xhoshad proclaims.

"Where?" I frown.

"The Bowels," Nerazi reiterates. "To enter, we must go down one of the ventilation shafts."

His announcement has me arching out of Seriq's hold. The emerald-eyed glow of his eyes narrows on me in warning.

"Hold still!" he hisses.

"No!" I snap. "We can't go down there—we'll get incinerated!"

"No we won't—" Xhoshad attempts to soothe, but I cut him off.

"I will!" I insist. "I'm not a bogeyman, er, bogeylady, or whatever the heck you are!"

"Vasura," Nerazi supplies.

"Either way, I die!"

"You won't die," Xhoshad promises. "It's safe for humans."

"How do you know?" I burst out.

Nerazi angles his bright neon gaze toward Xhoshad, as if curious to hear the answer—*that makes two of us.*

The red-eyed monster doesn't say anything for a moment before confessing, "I know someone—*a human*—who lives down there."

"Who?" I demand, not believing him entirely.

Seriq says something in their language, to which Nerazi replies in rapid-sounding surprise.

"What?!" I burst out, unsure if they're talking about what is after us.

"You'll see," Nerazi responds cryptically, and I want to pull my hair out.

I open my mouth to argue, but Seriq's arms tighten around my folded body, the only indication of our descent, before we plummet into the sweltering, black darkness below. It effectively silences me, a scream of terror caught in my throat. Up, up, up the temperature climbs as down, down, down we fall. I cling to Seriq, sure I'm tumbling to my death. Finally, we level out, shooting from the cloud of steam into a slightly cooler space. If possible, it seems even darker down here.

The volcanoes must not produce light like ours on Earth.

We float on for what seems like only a few more minutes until Seriq sets me down between Xhoshad and Nerazi. Their glowing eyes barely illuminate the area in front of us, but I think it's a door. Xhoshad calls out in their language, and the door slowly opens. A pair of strange eyes meets mine, and I wonder if it's a different type of monster. They're not as large and bright as my monsters, and there's something familiar about their hazel gleam....

"Alexis?!" the monster exclaims seconds before wrapping itself around my body.

I blink in confusion, too baffled to be afraid.

Why is the thing *hugging* me?

"I thought I'd never see you again! It's been so long, and things down here are so bad...."

My brain scrambles to process what is happening, when

my fingers brush against something on the monster's wrist. My brow wrinkles in recognition as I trace the charm I gave to my best friend eons ago.

And then it clicks.

The monster is Roxy.

SIXTEEN
Alexis

Pure joy erupts inside of me at the realization that Roxy is alive and well.

I embrace her against me in the same hug she tried to give me before, tears overflowing down my cheeks.

"How are you alive? How do you live down *here*?!"

Roxy draws me inside, talking to someone else in the monster tongue that mimics a snake to my ears. I marvel at her ability to replicate the sounds, but then again, she's lived here for over ten years. Over time, it makes sense that she would learn to speak their language, and her eyes would change, too. I try not to dwell on that too much. Truthfully, her enlarged, glowing orbs freak me out.

A lot.

Looking around the darkness, all I see are the three familiar pairs of eyes, along with Roxy's, when a fourth monstrous gaze joins the others. His eyes are a fiery orange, and I instinctively cringe back from its intensity. The newcomer hisses something at me. Seriq steps up to my back, pulling me securely into his embrace as Xhoshad stands to my right and Nerazi to my left.

"Alexis, this is Rastorj, your friend's mate. He is welcoming you into his home," Xhoshad explains.

I stretch forward to catch Roxy's illuminated eyes.

"Mate?!"

She sighs, asking my monsters something. Back and forth they go for about a minute before Xhoshad gives a curt nod, following Rastorj. Nerazi does the same, as does Seriq, who pauses to run a finger down the mark on my neck—*his mark*. I can't tell if he's still in his shadow form or corporal form, but I panic when they leave.

"It's ok," Roxy calms. "They're just giving us some space for me to do this."

At her words, a flame blazes to life.

Fire.

"Ahhhhh!" I sigh in relief, drinking in the beautiful sight of light.

My eyelids flutter, spasming into use once more, as I look around. The room is large with a high, vaulted ceiling, but the space is just basically the inside of a cave. There is a crude table on one side and what appears to be some pillows and a rug in another corner, similar to something I've seen in the Middle East. Roxy is near the resting area, swallowed in the shadows as if avoiding the light. Now that I can see her clearly, her eyes remind me of a doll's, too large for her face, making her look cutesy and eerie at the same time.

"Are you ok?" I wonder at the pinched look on her face.

"Yes, the light hurts me," she explains. "It's why the others left. They can't tolerate any light. Over the years, my eyes have obviously adapted to living here. The very air in Vasuriad is full of sinqol, which makes it possible for the eyes to absorb more light. At least, that's how Rastorj described it to me."

"And Rastorj is your.... *mate*?"

Roxy hums in answer, shrugging her left shoulder over to display a smooth, white scar carved into an intricate pattern into her flesh.

"This is my mating mark," she announces proudly.

"Rox—that's gorgeous, but I'm confused...."

My best friend from a lifetime ago sighs.

"I know; I'll try to explain as much as I can, but we only have half an hour until the candle is spent. I won't light anymore tonight. Honestly, the longer you're in the dark, the quicker your eyes will adjust. We did you a disservice by lighting it, but your mates knew you were missing it."

I'm touched by their thoughtfulness and Roxy's, especially seeing how much discomfort burning it causes her.

"Thank you. I have missed the light."

"Yeah, it takes awhile getting used to, but eventually, your sight returns. Your other senses become stronger, too. My hearing is superb compared to when I lived back on Earth. I can hear a scurion long before they show up."

"A what now?"

"A scurion. Imagine a spider mixed with a crocodile with no eyes that can hunt you with smell and sound alone."

I recoil back in horror.

"I don't want to imagine that!" I shriek. "What the hell, Roxy! What do you mean before they show up? Do those things live down here?!"

She nods.

"Yep, and they're not even the worst of the monstrous creatures down here."

She tucks a strand of her long, brown hair back, drawing

my eyes to the fact that she's wearing some sort of short tunic with no sleeves. She catches me staring.

"Don't worry. Rastorj is getting you one. He'll leave it in the hall for me to retrieve in a moment."

Another sigh escapes me.

"Thanks. To say I'm out of my comfort zone is putting it lightly, but I don't get it, Roxy. Why do you live down here if it's so dangerous? And so freaking hot!"

She chuckles.

"Because we have no choice. If we want to live, we have to do so in the harshest conditions, but my mate protects me. And is it really any hotter than Texas?"

"Scarily enough, yes—and that place is like Satan's taint, according to one meme."

Roxy shakes her head.

"A meme—I haven't thought of those things in forever. I've forgotten a lot about home."

She says this last bit without any bitterness, just an acknowledgment of the truth.

"Don't you miss it?" I venture.

Shrugging, she taps her lip, trying to put words to her thoughts.

"It's been a long time since I've spoken English, too," she chuckles. "I didn't realize I don't even think in it anymore until you showed up. God, I've missed you. What took you so long to get here?"

My mind boggles at her question.

"I don't even know how to answer that. First, tell me if you miss home."

"Not like you think. Yes, I miss Earth—mostly my parents and friends—but so much time has passed. I couldn't go back knowing what it would do to Rastorj."

"What would it do?" I wonder.

"Kill him," comes her automatic response. "Vasura can't be without their mates. They need us to live like we need air to breathe."

And just like that, the weight of her words comes crashing down upon my shoulders. I shake my head in denial, not wanting to be the reason whether my monsters live or die.

"What's wrong?" Roxy prompts, inching closer to me, shielding her eyes from the tiny candle flame.

"Everything," I laugh humorlessly.

She nods sadly.

"You never did tell me what took you so long to get here."

"I have no clue what you mean by that."

"What happened after your mates took me?"

"They aren't my mates," I refute, making Roxy snort.

"Don't tell them that," she teases.

"I ran," I confess. "I moved to Australia and never came back until...."

"Until what?"

"My dad was sick."

"Is he ok now?"

Numbly, I shake my head.

"No....he died a few days ago. I saw him for maybe two hours—two hours from the twelve years that I'd been gone."

"What about your mom?"

I flinch at the question.

"She died a year after you were taken."

"You didn't come home?" she asks without rancor, and I just shake my head.

"I was too scared. I blamed myself for what happened to you. No one believed me, of course, but I didn't know how to fix it—how to save you without confronting them again."

There's a shuffling noise in the hall. Roxy walks out of the room and comes back seconds later with a coarse-looking tunic in her hand, which I gratefully take and slip over my head. The rough, dark gray material stops at the apex of my thighs, barely covering enough to be decent. Then again, I'm a few inches taller than Roxy, so it makes sense that what stops at mid-thigh on her wouldn't be the same for me.

"Well, I'm glad you're here now. I won't lie, I thought you would've showed up a long time ago, but it's not the best down here...."

"You keep saying that. What are you hiding from that has you living in Hell's Crapper?"

Roxy laughs.

"An apt name for The Bowels. And not what are we hiding from, but *who*—and that would be The Fallacious."

"The Fallacious?"

Roxy nods.

"Yes, the false king. Think about Emperor Nero and multiply that by ten."

I cringe.

"Oh, god, that sounds—"

"Fucking horrible?" She cuts me off acrimoniously. "Trust me, if there were any way to live on Earth with Rastorj, we would have split a long time ago, but it's just not an option. And I won't leave him!"

She yells this last part, and I know it's for her mate's benefit and not mine. I smile at her.

"You love him," I state simply, seeing the truth.

"I really do, even if...."

"Even if what?"

Roxy turns away, and I walk over to place a tentative

hand on her back. She leans into my touch, and I wrap my arms around her in a comforting hug.

"I'm barren."

Her words make me frown.

"Barren? Like—"

"I can't get pregnant."

Snorting, I wonder how to respond.

"Rox....I don't think you're barren; I think you're trying to get pregnant with the wrong person."

She shushes me, looking hastily over her shoulder.

"Don't say that—you'll hurt his feelings!"

"I'm sorry—I didn't mean any offense, but they're a completely different species! How can either of you expect you to get pregnant?"

Roxy relaxes at this.

"Oh, I see. You don't think Rastorj shouldn't be my mate, but that Vasura can't get humans pregnant. They can," she clarifies.

"And you know this how?"

"Because of the Lost Heir," she hums before continuing. "Vasura are born of dissolute human emotions. They literally exist only because of our kind. As they grew into existence, so did their monstrous realm. Over time, they grew independent of humans, although still wholly dependent upon them for food. Vasura are like energy vampires, for lack of other words, they feed off your feelings. The more potent and depraved, the better, hence why they scare humans. Fear is like an aphrodisiac to the Vasura. But over time, humans have become less and less afraid of them. Eventually, only children feared them, and even then, that number was dwindling. It was around this time that the old king learned that they could breed with human women.

Before this, Vasura had only been born from a human emotion and were always men."

"How did he learn this?" I cut in.

"He found his mate," Roxy says simply. "She called to him just like you called to your mates."

"I didn't call to them," I grumble.

"You did," she insists. "Back to the story. The old king found his human mate and impregnated her. According to the tale, she gave birth to the first female Vasura—*the lost heir.*"

A chill prickles the flesh on my arms.

"And where is this hybrid bogeybaby?"

Roxy grins at my term.

"Lost. No one knows. At the time the baby was born, The Fallacious was rising against the old king, trying to take his throne. The human woman fled back to Earth with her child for her safety after her mate was slaughtered. Now, everyone awaits the return of the rightful heir to overthrow the tyrant that now rules."

I let her words digest, feeling sad for this lost heir.

"And what if the heir doesn't want to return or rule?"

Roxy's eyes fill with tears.

"Then all the Vasura will die. They need to find their human mates to live, but The Fallacious won't let them use the portals anymore to go into the human world. Lex—their kind is slowly dying, literally starving to death."

"And does anyone even have any clue as to who this Lost Heir might even be?"

My best friend looks into my eyes, her overly large hazel ones filled with premonition.

"*You.*"

SEVENTEEN
Seriq

I pace impatiently, waiting for my mate to be done chatting.

Xhoshad reminds me that Alexis needs this reunion, needs time to adjust, but my body won't settle until she's completely ours.

Completely mine.

For twelve long human years, I've risked death by visiting the portal that takes me to her room. Only my cunning and ruthlessness have kept me alive—and the desperate need to be with Alexis. After what seemed like an eternity, I sensed her presence once more in the old house. The very dust of the rundown place carried her unique fragrance to my nostrils—along with the scent of her lust and coupling with another.

The same human from before.

Even just thinking about the man has the saliva pooling in my mouth. Thoughts of ripping him to shreds with my teeth and claws dance in my mind. I will hunt him down and when I find him, I will show him *no* fucking mercy. He stole what is *mine*. The mental reminder that the human scum took my mate's innocence is enough to send me into a frenzy—but that he touched her *again*.

And she let him.

Xhoshad would tell me I'm being foolish, that humans don't understand our concept of mates, but Alexis knows—knew—who she belongs to. She's just been running from that truth for over a decade. I pause when I hear her tinkling laugh come from the other room and growl, wanting to see her happy face, devoid of the intoxicating emotions my kind feeds off. Her fear, anger, lust, and sadness are delicious, but I don't want those things for my mate.

Except lust.

She can feel that for the rest of her days, and I will feast like a king off her pleasure. Her anger is piquant, a spicy flavor that amuses me, but her fear and sadness are like ashes on my tongue. I don't savor them in the least and would much prefer to taste her happiness. A healthy mate is a happy mate, and Alexis must be healthy to carry my baby. My cock swells at the thought of her soft stomach rounded with my child.

Soon.

"Seriq," Xhoshad calls. "How long have you been visiting the portal?"

"A while," I answer vaguely.

I rarely speak in more than one to three words. It gets my point across well enough, and the others rarely try to engage me in tiresome conversation. I have one reason to exist—*and she's sitting in the other room*. At the thought of Alexis, my mind begins the familiar chant of *mine, mine, mine*. My muscles twitch and flex as I bodily restrain myself from charging into the lit room and stealing her back into the darkness. To do so would be foolish, though. Alexis needs this moment with her friend, and the light could blind me for hours, perhaps even days.

Leaving me vulnerable if The Fallacious or his Revenant Swarm attacked.

Snarling, I rake my claws down the side of the stone wall, sparks spurting forth, making me wince in pain at their brightness.

"Knock it off!" Nerazi snaps, just as restless and edgy.

The mating call is riding us harder than Xhoshad. The cruder the base emotion a Vasura is formed from, the wilder, more violent, and uncivilized he is. Greed is a nasty instigator, but possession is another level of selfishness that Nerazi can't compete with—what he feels is ten times stronger inside of me. I glare at my yellow-eyed friend, noting his miraculous return to health. Another day or so and he would have slipped into the abyss of nothingness. Xhoshad might be pissed that I returned to the portal, but it saved Nerazi's life. As egocentric as I am, I still worried for my brothers, but I was largely driven by my unstoppable determination to find and claim my mate. Now that I found her, I'm sick of waiting.

I want her underneath me, begging for more, as I fuck her senseless.

I raise my hand to scratch the wall again in the same one-clawed imitation as the mating mark I left on Alexis, when Xhoshad abruptly stands.

"Rastorj," he addresses the Vasura with bright purple eyes, "can we rest here in the caverns for a time? We must...."

Rastorj nods.

"I understand the demands of a mating claim. I will take Roxy out hunting for a few days to give you some privacy. I welcome the arrival of your mate. Mine is.... lonely for a friend."

The confession costs him greatly. Rastorj is formed from conceit, an emotion that needs no one, but by claiming Roxy, he's adjusted to cater to her every whim. I meant it when I told Alexis she is our queen. I will strive every day to grant all her wishes. *I will kill for her, bleed for her, die for her.* Unfortunately, there will be some things I can't do—like return her to the human world. Aside from the fact Vasura can't live there, I would surely kill the man who dared touch what is mine. Alexis would be devastated, something I loathe to admit, even to myself. She has *feelings* for this human filth.

But I will erase every memory of him.

In time, she will only cry out my name—and that moment is quickly approaching. Baring my teeth at Xhoshad, I tell him without words I'm done waiting. I want Alexis *now*; either he can go get her or suffer the consequences of me doing it. My red-eyed friend is much more cautious and tactful than either Nerazi or me. He will be able to lure Alexis into the darkness where we can pounce on her like the feral beasts we are. The thought makes me chuckle evilly, and Nerazi shoots me an intrigued look. The troublemaker is always down for causing mischief.

Xhoshad prowls down the hall, keeping to the shadows, calling out Alexis' name. Her friend rounds the corner, relief on her face. Years spent in the pitch-black Bowels has made her sensitive to the light. Clothing and candles are small gifts Rastorj accorded his mate, but she has little use for either in our world. Although, I appreciate the covering Roxy shared with Alexis. I don't relish the thought of another male—of any species—seeing my mate naked. The rounded splendor of her flesh is for my eyes only, as well as

Nerazi and Xhoshad. Thoughts of Alexis nude and in my arms tightens my loins painfully.

Where is she?

"Alexis wonders if....I can stay with her for the nigh—" Roxy begins, but I cut her off.

"No," I bark decisively.

I've waited long enough.

Roxy gulps, cowering a bit at my brusqueness that has Rastorj snarling at me.

"Apologies," I bow to Roxy, and then her offended mate. "I am eager."

Rastorj nods in understanding, mollified by my apology, but Nerazi and Xhoshad stare at me like I've grown two heads. Rarely do I dignify to speak in complete sentences, but I don't want to make enemies of Alexis' only friend here. Roxy hesitates, coming to stand by her mate, before she asks:

"Does Alexis know what you plan?"

Nerazi wrinkles his brow at the question.

"Yes," he responds.

"But does she understand what it entails—have you explained it to her? She's very confused about.... her reasoning for being here." Roxy pauses to laugh. "I remember when she first told me about you three. It was immediately evident that you wanted her, but Alexis can be a little obtuse. I just don't think she gets what's going on. If you tell her, she might be more cooperative."

"*Might be?*" Xhoshad chokes.

Roxy shrugs.

"You know Alexis—well, we *knew* Alexis—but I doubt much has changed in ten years. She can be stubborn, remember?"

I recall very well how willful she could be. That brazenness that has grown into defiance I can't wait to discipline out of her. Nerazi, Xhoshad, and I exchange a glance, talking without speaking. Yes, Alexis deserves answers, but I'm more a man of action. I know what Alexis needs, even if she doesn't. I can smell her arousal, demanding that I take her, once and for all. There will be time for explanations afterwards. I cross my arms over my chest, firmly projecting my feelings to the other two. Nerazi is on board, but Xhoshad is soft where our mate is concerned. Roxy senses the tension and quickly leaves to get Alexis.

Her cry of dismay when the candle is extinguished tugs at my heart, but she can have light another day. Roxy leads her slowly and steadily into my embrace. She whispers my name, snuggling into my chest, and I repress the urge to throw back my head and roar in victory. Alexis might be angry and afraid, but her actions tell me that she does trust us. I stroke her long, wavy hair, calming her without words. Roxy and her mate whisper goodnight before leaving us alone. I continue to hold onto Alexis, letting Nerazi and Xhoshad know I'm staking my claim first.

As the leader of our trium, Xhoshad had first right to mark our mate, but the strongest gets to breed and claim her first. No one will contest that's me. My base emotion eclipses Nerazi's, and although both are founded in avarice, mine is kissed with a hint of mania—*making me both unhinged and unpredictable.* My psychotic disposition didn't endear me to many other Vasura, but after The Fallacious came into power, my kind started to band together. Xhoshad and Nerazi were already a team when they stumbled across me. The three of us are a family in the human sense, working together to find a mate to share, but they know who I am at the core. I can't contain it.

I won't.

Sweeping Alexis into my arms, I cradle her gently against me as I take her to a large sleeping den. Rastorj has done much to see to his mate's comforts—*no easy feat in The Bowels*—and I'm grateful for the space. I lay Alexis down on the sleeping pad, my large hand splaying across her flat stomach, pinning her in place. She trembles under my touch in both awareness and nervousness. For her, this is all happening too fast, but for me, it's been an eternity—*a living hell*—to not see her, touch her, fuck her.

When Xhoshad first linked the portal to her room, Nerazi and I didn't come. Our red-eyed leader was testing to see if she was even a viable option, feeding off of her fear and tasting whether she would be our mate. Once he learned that Alexis indeed was our destined one, he set out to gain her trust instead of just consume her emotions. Only when he was convinced our mate would not run did he introduce Nerazi, who could barely restrain him from taking her then, but Xhoshad insisted we wait until she was of human age—which is why I didn't visit her until she was eighteen. I knew I couldn't wait three years to have what I wanted immediately.

The irony of it all now.

Poor Alexis has been thrown into our world and given mere hours to come to terms with the fact that the three of us are claiming her as our mate. Me, on the other hand, I've been waiting for this moment for forever. Reaching up, I rend the scratchy, offensive material concealing her body in half. My woman should be bare beneath me—*will be bare*. Xhoshad hisses in warning, reminding me that I will owe Rastorj and his mate some new human coverings, but I don't care. All I can think about is the expanse of creamy skin spread out before me like a sumptuous feast. Her full breasts are tipped with rosy nipples that my claws toy with delicately, earning a shudder from my mate.

My lips curl up at the sight, but I won't be content until she's screaming my name. Pinning her hands above her head, I lean in close to her face. Alexis' breaths are more like panting hiccups, and the scent of her arousal slams into me. She squirms under my gaze, fighting me still, and all the blood rushes straight to my cock. She needs to be punished —*wants to be punished*—and I am just the one to do it. Xhoshad appears at my elbow, whispering something in our tongue in my ear. I hiss at his request to fuck Alexis first. I am the strongest—*it is my right*—but he warns I might be too rough and hurt her.

I frown, gazing down at the beautiful woman waiting for me to fill her. In the darkness, my eyes easily can see the wetness glistening between her pink folds. Releasing my long tongue, I lick up some of the moisture, growling at the taste of her. Xhoshad is wrong. I will be rough, but I won't hurt—I couldn't if I tried. Alexis is my mate, and I'm bound to ensure her safety, even from myself. At the same time, I acknowledge Xhoshad has a different bond with her—one that predates both mine and Nerazi's—but that doesn't make his request to breed her first more valid. He might have marked her first, and we all might be sharing her, but make no mistake.

Alexis is mine.

CHAPTER EIGHTEEN
Alexis

Seriq's incandescent emerald eyes bore into mine, the pupil-less depths conveying a message too overwhelming for me to address. Everything in my life has boiled down to this moment in time it feels like. Before, when they marked me, it was just a precursor of what was to come. Spread now beneath Seriq's weight, I'm on the precipice—once I fall over this ledge, there'll be no going back. I bite my lower lip in apprehension, deciding whether to beg my monsters to continue....or to stop. My body chooses for me, arching up into Seriq's tongue, silently pleading for more.

Apparently, he was right—*my body already knows what my heart wants.*

Refusing to acknowledge that a monster knows me better than I know myself, I close my eyes and relish the sensations of Seriq licking me languorously. I propel my hips forward, impaling myself on the long length of his tongue which he curls deep inside my pussy, eliciting an indecent moan from my lips. His sharp claws scuff against the tender flesh at my nipples, sending sparks of agony intermingled with ecstasy throughout my body. Seriq doesn't stop until he lashes an explosive orgasm from my core. Only then does he ease back, ever assessing me.

"One down," he murmurs, and I gasp.

"What does *that* mean?" I pant.

Of course, the taciturn bastard doesn't reply. Xhoshad shoulders his way in front of me, earning a furious snarl from Seriq, which he ignores.

"It means you're not ready to take our cocks," the red-eyed bogeyman announces.

"I know I'm not! I've been trying to tell you tha—"

Nerazi chuckles from somewhere in the room, but I can't see because his eyes aren't facing me.

"You misunderstand, little mate, he meant physically, not mentally. We just need your pussy to be wetter and wider—coming a dozen or so times should easily remedy it."

My eyes bulge at this.

I think twelve orgasms might be overkill but I've seen their dicks, and Nerazi is right—I'm going to be stretched and stuffed. The thought makes me tingly, and I wonder how much of their cocks I can take. I'm so small in comparison. Seriq yanks Xhoshad aside, and apprehension wars with my lust. Everything is moving so quickly—physically, I want this, but mentally, I'm not ready.

"Stop thinking," Seriq directs. "Just feel."

I bite my lower lip so hard I taste blood as I struggle internally on what to do, but Nerazi makes that decision for me. From a distance, he reaches out with shadowy tendrils and once more pins my hands above my head. He holds me down for Seriq, but at the same time, slips wispy fingers to thread through mine, cupping my palm against his. Startled, my eyes fly to meet his amber glow. The gesture is as erotic as it is sweet.

Maybe the mischievous man has a softer side of him I don't know.

All thoughts flee my head when Seriq's tongue comes out to trace the single claw mark he made into my neck. He snakes it up the left side of my throat, looping it around like a necklace down the other side. There, he flicks the forked tip against my right nipple. All the while, his eyes never leave mine. His taloned hands grab my hips, brushing the head of his massive cock against the sensitive folds of my pussy. With his own shadows, Seriq slips the smoky extension between us, circling my clit. More shadow limbs join the others, this time from Xhoshad, caressing me everywhere. It's like sensory overload, my mind fracturing and splintering until....

I shatter.

My loud cry ricochets around the cavernous room as my orgasm slams into me by complete surprise. I feel like I've run a marathon, my chest heaving in exaggerated exertion. The rise and fall of my breasts is mesmerizing as Seriq licks first the right nipple, and then the left. The aloof monster gives me a moment to recover before beginning again. As one, Xhoshad and Nerazi help the crimson-eyed magician work his magic over me. As promised, they don't stop until I come twelve times. By this point, I swear my bones have dissolved, and I'm nothing but a puddle of pleasure.

"Now you're ready," Nerazi hisses, still holding me down with his shadow hands.

Both he and Xhoshad are keeping some distance between them and me, and I know it's because Seriq is so possessive. While the green-eyed demon obviously doesn't mind sharing, he's made it evident that he wants to have me first. Curling his tongue back into his mouth, I can barely make out the glint of his sharp teeth from the glow of his eyes, but I see them curve upward in conquest.

"Mine," he snarls, and it's the only warning I get before he surges forward, forcing the thick, mushroomed head of his dick inches into my dripping core.

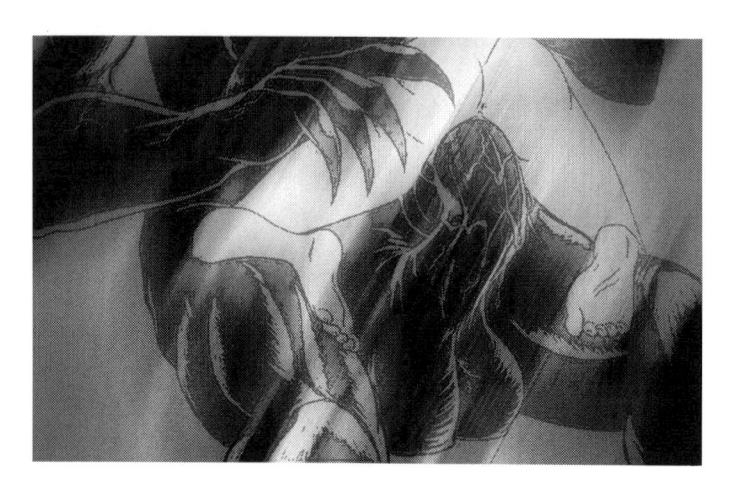

My eyes flutter closed as my pussy spasms against the intrusion. Slowly and carefully, Seriq continues to edge deeper inside of me. When he's halfway there, I yank out of Nerazi's shadow grasp and attempt to sit up. Xhoshad withdraws his smoky touch as Seriq leans down over me, his lumbering form angling close. My eyes have adjusted enough that I can make out shadows once more from the glow of their eyes.

"It's too much," I whimper.

"You're not wet enough," Seriq whispers into my ear.

Not wet enough?

I'm fucking *gushing*.

The emerald-eyed monster changes positions so that I'm riding him and can better regulate the pace. I'm surprised he's conceding any control, but he keeps his large hands around my waist to guide me as I try to seat myself upon his massive cock.

"Let me help," Nerazi offers, and I narrow my eyes at his glowing yellow ones.

Nerazi pretends to be courteous, but a wicked demon hides behind that devilishly charming smile. He steps into my space, his monstrous cock pulsating inches from the side of my face. Unconsciously, I lick my lips, the tip of my tongue brushing over the sensitive head of Nerazi's dick. It twitches, as does his mouth.

Fucker.

He only came over to help *himself*.

Something that Xhoshad already knows because he's ordering Nerazi out of the way and comes floating over. A shiver, part from fear and part from excitement, courses through my frame as the red-eyed monster takes in my exposed pussy filled with Seriq's cock. Xhoshad's ruby eyes lick a scorching path of desire from the top of my head to the center of my spread legs. Under his heated stare, I grow wetter and wetter.

But apparently, *not wet enough*.

I wait breathlessly to see what Xhoshad plans. To my surprise, he recedes back into the darkness of the room, and my shoulders slump in equal measures of relief and disappointment. I wonder what he would have done....

My gasp echoes around the stillness of the dark.

I can barely see Xhoshad's scarlet eyes from the corner where he's tucked himself into, *but I can feel him*. Becoming one with shadows, he reaches out with numerous limbs to grab me. First my right arm, then my left one. Then my right leg, and lastly my left leg. His shadow hands pin mine behind my back, thrusting my breasts upward. Nerazi growls hungrily, but doesn't dare come closer. Xhoshad then works the shadows to spread my legs even wider as the ghost of a hand comes to caress my throat.

Before squeezing it.

It's not painful, but I can feel my airway slowly becoming constricted—just like when I'm having a panic attack—but for some reason, this doesn't send me into a spiral. If anything, it turns me on *more*. What once scared me now empowers me. I arch into Xhoshad's shadow, feeling him claim me with just this touch. I silently urge him to press harder, and he complies with my unspoken wish. Just as white spots begin to dance into my vision, signaling my impending blackout, another shadow hand snakes out to touch me.

Right where I crave it most.

In tandem, Xhoshad's wispy tendrils garrote my throat while the other encircles my clit roughly. The white spots return, but instead of passing out, I seem to rise above, floating higher and higher into a plane of pure ecstasy. I toss my head back and slam my hands on Seriq's chest, the movement fully seating me upon him at last. A feral growl escapes his lips as he begins to fuck me in earnest, the motion bobbing my breasts up and down. From the shadows, Nerazi reaches out with one smoky sliver to tweak my nipples. I gasp at the sensation, my muscles clenching, making my pussy clamp even tighter around Seriq. His groans spill into the room.

"Mine. Mine. Mine. MINE!" he chants, the sound a rising crescendo as he comes deep within me.

I can feel his hot seed coating my walls before dripping down the sides of his throbbing cock and escaping out of my pussy. Spurt after spurt, Seriq fills me up, and I twitch before collapsing on top of his chest. We rest there, both of us recovering our breath while the other two still simply just watch, and I wonder what they're waiting for.

"Alexis Stanton," Seriq intones, and I startle against him.

I'm not used to him speaking, and I didn't know he knew my *full* name.

"I claim you as my mate. With this mark and my seed—" he pauses to scoop up some of his cum, bringing it to his face so I see the bright green droplets before smearing it over the spot he etched into my flesh, "you are *mine*."

Both Nerazi and Xhoshad whisper something in their hissing tongue as I feel something spark to life inside of me before slowly fading away.

"Wh-what was that?" I whisper in a shaky voice.

Seriq grins at me.

"The beginning."

Again, I shiver at his ambiguous words. I might've been wrong—the green-eyed monster is turning out to be more troublesome than Nerazi—and I think I've bitten off more than I can chew. This is proven when Seriq leisurely starts propelling his hips upward, gaining speed with every thrust.

"What are you doing?!" I pant, not sure my body can take any more.

In answer, Seriq slams into me hard, ripping a scream crossed between pain and pleasure from my lips. He pauses, his head tipped questioningly, and I know he's waiting to see if I'm alright. I open my mouth to tell him I need a break, but my traitorous hips buck forward, a plea for him to continue. He waits a moment, his green eyes blazing into mine, before complying. Shadow tendrils snake out from his body, the smoky wisps caressing me tenderly—a stark contrast to the rough thrust of his pelvis grinding against mine.

From the darkness, Xhoshad and Nerazi watch. I can

feel their hunger grow, a sweet torment to Xhoshad, but agony for Nerazi, who always wants more. Silently, I countdown from five, not even getting to one, before my yellow-eyed monster launches out of the shadows to join us. A grim smirk curls my lips. Seriq doesn't share well—*and I love it.*

As predicted, he hisses at Nerazi and seats me even deeper on top of him. I feel my sensitive and bruised pussy contract against the invasion as I surge upward to relieve some of the pressure, but a pair of hands on my shoulders slams me back down. My cry of surprise and pain is muffled by Seriq's chest as I fall onto him completely once more. A snarl gathers in my throat—*a sign I've spent too much time with them already*—and I turn to snap at Nerazi, but the feel of something warm and wet on my ass makes me pause. I try to sit up, but the troublemaker keeps a hand pinned to my back so I can't move. I crane my head to the side, peering around Seriq's slab of muscles until I glimpse Nerazi's long tongue against the white globe of my left butt cheek. Our eyes lock, and I shiver at the blatant mischief stamped into his features.

Never breaking eye contact, Nerazi slowly shifts his tongue until it rests in the crevice between my ass. I gasp as he swirls the tip against the sensitive center before pushing in, inch by surprising inch. I bolt upright, sinking back down Seriq's massive length, squirming to dislodge Nerazi. All the movement does is shimmy me further on Seriq's dick, his girth nearly splitting me in two.

"What are you doing?" I hiccup as a strange cocktail of emotions bombards my body, apprehension, lust, and anticipation fizzing in my gut.

"Mmmm, preparing you," Nerazi hums, never once removing his tongue where it's fucking my ass.

"Pr-pr-preparing me for what?" I stammer as Seriq angles his hips up and down.

"My cock," Nerazi purrs.

My mind blanks.

"I can't take you there!"

Nerazi pauses in his ministrations.

"Why not? You're fully seated on Seriq—and he's the biggest of the three of us."

My cheeks heat at his words.

"Well, vags stretch—assholes don't."

The evil monster snakes his tongue back inside, making me squeal.

"Sure feels like it stretches," he comments.

I swallow thickly.

"I've....I've never done *that*," I admit in a whisper.

Seriq hisses at my confession, but Nerazi gets in his face.

"Back off! You've made your claim—you can't be her first at everything," he spits.

"Don't remind me of the human scum," Seriq snarls, and I stare in consternation.

Is he still upset that I slept with Mark first after all these years?

Hissed bickering pulls me back, and I try to figure out what the two monsters are arguing about, but Xhoshad glides over and stops them.

"Alexis is all of ours. We'll compromise. Nerazi—you can have her ass first, but Seriq can fuck her at the same time," he decrees, and Nerazi immediately begins to argue once more.

"How will I fully fuck her if Seriq's fat cock is already deep inside her?"

A good question.

"Thrust in when he pulls out," Xhoshad suggests.

My eyes bulge at the idea. Surely, they'll tear me apart, but the three of them don't seem concerned.

I'm about to die, but it's one hell of a way to go.

Nerazi's lips brush my ear as he leans down and scoops up some of Seriq's cum. He brings the brightly colored droplets to my lips to taste before ringing my ass with his cum-drenched fingers. Carefully, he inserts one at a time, stopping at three. My heart is beating faster than a hummingbird's wings as my brain tries to assimilate the sensations. As he pulls back, Seriq surges forward. When Seriq edges away, Nerazi thrusts his fingers back in. They continue this pattern until I feel myself spiraling toward yet another orgasm.

Just as I'm about to crash over the edge, Nerazi removes his fingers *and replaces it with his engorged dick.*

My shrill scream rends the air, and to my utter surprise, I come hard. My pussy and ass compress inward, wringing a groan from both monsters. Finally, my ass releases, and I relax into Nerazi's touch as my pussy flutters intensely around Seriq's girth. They give me a moment before the two of them start fucking me again in earnest. In swift jabs, Seriq jackhammers into my pussy, the thick circumference of his dick grating against my clit whenever he pulls back, and Nerazi mirrors him in my ass.

I dig my nails into Seriq's chest, desperately clinging to him so I don't fly into pieces. Just when I think I'm about to explode, the green-eyed monster pulls out completely, and Nerazi unloads deep inside of my ass. I fall forward, but Seriq's shadow limbs catch me. In the faint glow of his eyes, I can see him working his dick with his hands. Within seconds, rope after rope of green cum erupts forth, covering his stomach. I lean forward, laving my tongue over his saturated abs.

I'll never get enough of him—of his taste.

Behind me, Nerazi leans forward to whisper in his tongue. Seriq and Xhoshad echo him, and the same feeling as before with Seriq lights up my body—a tingling awareness that sizzles down through me and then fades away.

"My turn," Xhoshad calls, and I swear my thighs quiver at his announcement.

"I don't know how much more I can take," I confess.

The red-eyed monster gently pulls me away from Nerazi and Seriq. Something cool comes to touch between my legs and I startle before realizing he's cleaning me. I ease into Xhoshad's care, feeling like a limp noodle.

"We can wait," he says, and I catch a hint of sadness.

Recalling the words both Seriq and Nerazi spoke, I realize this is something important to Xhoshad. I bite my lip, unsure of what to do.

"I can use my hands and mouth," I offer huskily, the thought lighting up my center once more.

Xhoshad hums in acknowledgement, coming forward to bring the tip of his dick to my lips. I open my mouth, taking in the wide head, flicking it back and forth with my tongue before enclosing my mouth around him. Using my teeth, I lightly skim down the sides, making Xhoshad hiss in pleasure. The faster I work him, the more turned on I get. Squirming to relieve the tension blossoming between my legs, I grip my scarlet-eyed monster's cock with both hands, pumping up and down.

Moaning, Xhoshad fists my hair, yanking roughly and taking control of my movements. Before I know it, I'm mewling hungrily, dry humping the air as I greedily get my mouth fucked.

"It looks like you're ready for another round," he comments.

Cupping my ass, he spreads my legs wide, and Xhoshad rises to stand between them. Nerazi holds me at the perfect height for Xhoshad's dick to pierce my exposed pussy. In a single, smooth motion, he surges in, filling me completely. I inhale sharply at the invasion, the breath lodging in my throat at the feeling. Seriq joins us to my right, his tongue coming to lick my right nipple while Nerazi teases my left with his. The three of them work as a unit to bring me to a final orgasm before Xhoshad unleashes powerfully within me.

"I claim you, now and forever—my mate," he grits out between the pulsing of his dick.

Seriq and Nerazi say their piece, and something inside of my body shifts into place that I didn't know was missing. For one moment, an overwhelming feeling of love and contentment fills my senses. Xhoshad steps back, a smug look of satisfaction gleaming in his eyes, and I impulsively reach forward to grab his sensitive cock. His massive girth is still throbbing, and the tip is wet with his cum. Swiping it with my hand, I bring it to my eyes, squinting to see the blood-red drops from the glow of Nerazi's eyes, who's looking over my shoulder down at me.

I taste him, just like I did with Seriq, savoring the spicy, unique flavor.

All three monsters groan, making me grin in sleepy fulfilment.

"Now, you're ours," Xhoshad comments, but I'm too tired and sated to argue.

Tomorrow I will tell them that fucking me—and giving me more orgasms in one session than my entire life—doesn't make me theirs.

Tomorrow....

NINETEEN
Xhoshad

The sound of screaming shatters my cocoon of bliss.

Instinctively, I dissolve into shadows, covering my mate to protect her. Nerazi and Seriq follow suit, but what barrels through the door isn't what I expect. It's Roxy, Rastorj's mate. She's sobbing hysterically, and the sound rouses Alexis from her sleep. My beautiful mate sits up, her light hair a heavy curtain over her face that she absentmindedly pushes away. Squinting, she tries to pierce the darkness, concern creasing her forehead.

"Roxy, is that you? What's wrong?!"

"It's Rastorj—he's been attacked!" her friend cries.

"By what?" Nerazi demands.

The Bowels hold all sorts of unthinkable creatures, that Rastorj and Roxy lived down here for ten years is impressive. The two of them have been thriving, building a home and hunting the beasts that make most Vasura cringe—but not Rastorj. He is a hulking behemoth nearly a foot taller than Seriq, who is nine feet high. Whatever attacked Roxy's mate must be twice as big *and* twice as strong. I watch Alexis' friend fall to her knees in sorrow, her body shaking convulsively when she answers:

"It was the Revenant Swarm!"

Next to me, Alexis shrinks back at this.

"The Fallacious' Army?" she murmurs.

Startled, I gaze down upon her, my glowing eyes taking in her fearful countenance.

When did she learn about The Fallacious?

"Quick," I bark at Nerazi and Seriq, "go help Rastorj! I will stay with Roxy and Alexis."

The two of them nod before dispersing into smoky wisps and flitting away. My mate scrambles off the sleeping pad. I chase after her, but she's just going to her friend. Wrapping an arm around Roxy, Alexis murmurs quietly to her that everything will be alright, but this makes the other human woman wail even harder. I'm unsure if it was just a hollow human platitude meant to soothe her friend, or if Alexis really has no clue about what the Revenant Swarm is and who controls it. I sift over when I catch the sheen of tears on her cheeks.

"What's wrong?" I gently ask.

At first she doesn't answer, but I remember Alexis well. It takes her a bit to open up. As Roxy said, she doubts Alexis has changed overly, but twelve years is a long time in the human world. I watched my mate turn from a girl into a young woman, but I didn't see her grow completely into maturity. I feel like I know Alexis, but need more time to assess whether the ghost of her memory is accurate or just something I clung onto. Losing her all those years ago was devastating for my trium. Seriq, Nerazi, and I would reminisce about our girl because facing the truth—that she ran away—was too painful.

For Seriq, it was maddening. He had no control anymore because we had no idea where Alexis went. All the portals had been shut down and were being monitored, so we couldn't test them to try to find a way to our mate. The green-eyed Vasura wasn't giving up, though, and clearly snuck back to Alexis' childhood room in the hopes she would someday return. I had given up hope—as did Nerazi—but Seriq wouldn't.

Couldn't.

His base emotion was like a maggot eating him from the inside out. His possessive nature kept spurring him to find Alexis until he did. The miracle of seeing her after so long will always be a bittersweet moment for me. Sweet because she finally had come home; bitter because I knew it was not safe. My fear is that we'll forever be hunted, forever on the run, and never at peace. I wanted my mate, but having her here now, I realize the heavy price she must pay for our selfishness. I cannot ease the darkness, but wish I could welcome her into my world properly. Instead, we must hide in the depths of my realm's Hell so one monstrous man doesn't find us.

I tuck a finger under Alexis' chin, tipping it up so she looks into my eyes as I wait for her to answer me. She leans into my touch, and my heart slams into my chest. My mate might be fighting her destiny, but not as hard as I thought she would. Even now, I can taste her loneliness and ache for the years she spent alone and scared. How those last few days before she ran deteriorated so quickly still baffles me. Once upon a time, Alexis feared me. In the beginning, she didn't know I wasn't there to feast on her emotions—or whatever humans think my kind does—but to claim her as our mate. For months, I worked hard to cultivate a friendship, which she eventually accepted.

Only then did Nerazi join me, and lastly Seriq, who couldn't keep his hunger at bay. I understand humans well enough to know that our mate was young—too young—and needed time. I didn't want to push her into anything she wasn't comfortable with. As time passed, she became aware of us not just as monsters, but as *men*. I acknowledge it was largely subconscious, but Alexis wanted us—I tasted her desire—and it wasn't for anyone else. We knew she had a human boyfriend, but Nerazi and I decided to give our mate time. Her mother was dying, and although their relationship was not good, we didn't want to take Alexis too soon.

Seriq, of course, disagreed.

The night that he fed into Alexis' pleasure while she touched herself was when he wanted to claim her. We fought and it almost disbanded our trium, but I managed to convince Seriq to stay and wait—something I regret to this day. In my infinite wisdom, I counseled the other two Vasura that Alexis would come to us. She already leaned on us for emotional support; there wasn't a shadow of a doubt in my mind that she would turn to us for her physical needs. Except, she didn't. The boyfriend that I thought was meaningless turned out not to be. Alexis rarely spoke of him and never had him over. She didn't spend her nights with him— she spent them with *us*.

And yet, she gave her innocence to him.

If only I had agreed to take her when Seriq wanted, but I can't change the past. The last twelve years have been humbling, reminding me not to assume or take anything for granted. I could guess why my mate is crying, but have learned it's better to ask and know for certain. When Alexis was young, I would listen to her talk for hours, her soft confession swallowed by the darkness and me. I tasted her pain, confusion, hurt, just as I can taste it now. It's a familiar flavor I take no pleasure in.

"Why are you crying?" I prompt when she still doesn't reply.

"Because Roxy is," she answers succinctly.

My forehead wrinkles in consternation. I've been among humankind since the beginning of time—*born of their hostilities and fears*—and tears weren't a sickness. They weren't a disease you could catch. Therefore, my mate is crying in sympathy, but I wonder if it is solely for her friend or if she's imagining what it would be like to lose one of us. The idea is like an ember, sparking hope deep within me. I yearn for the day that Alexis wants me as much as I need her. She is my very air, and I can't breathe without her.

"It will be alright," I repeat my mate's words from earlier. "Nerazi and Seriq will defeat this swarm as we did before and bring Rastorj back to heal."

I don't bother to mention that The Fallacious' army departed of its own accord, leaving Nerazi and me with more questions. I don't want to alarm the two females more. Leaning down, I cradle Alexis' back in a hug as she does the same to Roxy. Her need to touch her friend is something deeply ingrained within me, too. Perhaps it is all those years apart, but I want to constantly have a shadow hand on my mate.

I can't give her the chance to run again.

We sit in silence as Roxy's sobs abate, and I wonder how Seriq and Nerazi are faring. It's my hope that Rastorj is well enough to join the fight. Three Vasura are better than two, and everything helps when fighting against mindless beings controlled by a real monster. I internally shudder at the thought of The Fallacious. For thirty long years, he's reigned, destroying my kind one Vasura at a time. I've tried to figure out his end game, but nothing makes sense. As the humans say, there is strength in numbers, but things are not how they once were. Humans have evolved into the light while we must recede into the shadows. Our food source is dwindling as humans become more and more connected with their overpoweringly bright technologies that they never turn off.

Perhaps The Fallacious was born of scarcity and fears there will not be enough sustenance.

The thought makes me frown. It still wouldn't excuse his actions, even if his base emotion is warmongering. Once we learned that the Vasura could mate, all effort should've been given to us finding a human woman; instead, The Fallacious closed the portals. He sealed off our chances of survival. Only luck would have it that I found Alexis in time. I wonder how much would be different now if she hadn't run. Given the state of my realm, a part of me almost wishes Seriq never returned to search for her. The odds of him using the portal at the exact moment Alexis was in her room is a decree of fate, though.

There is no argument that she's meant to be ours.

Yet, these are perilous times. The few human mates that once lived in Vasuriad were taken by The Fallacious. When he could not breed them, he sucked them dry. My kind is like a metaphorical vampire—we live off of human emotions, consuming their energy, but if we take too much, the person will die. The false king stole the other Vasuras' mates before they were properly marked. He claimed them for his crown, allowing the males to fight for the chance to win them back, but The Fallacious doesn't fight fair.

He fights dirty.

He used his army to defeat the Vasura that stood up for their mates. They died, as did the females when they couldn't produce—raped and murdered instead of protected and cherished. The Vasura are not a kind race, but females are rare. We don't abuse them. The humans call us monsters, but The Fallacious is the true abomination. I won't let that happen to Alexis—even if it means returning her to the human world. Seriq will fight me, but the thought of losing our mate to the hand of the false king guts me. A scratching sound brings me out of my thoughts. Alexis perks up, too.

"Is that them?"

I shake my head, forgetting she can't see. I'm linked to Nerazi and Seriq as I am to Alexis. Vasura markings are similar to GPS—they help us track one another—and right now, I don't sense either of my trium nearby. Pulling Alexis aside, I help Roxy to her feet. Her mate returns and will likely need aid for his wounds, but the best medicine will be to have his female at his side.

"It's Rastorj," I tell both of them, opening the door and leading my mate and her friend to the gathering den, but what greets me there is a sight I've only heard whispered.

Clothed in human garb, his glowing blue eyes assessing us, stands The Fallacious. Atop his head, a tribal crown completes his devious appearance. He wears a smug smile that makes me uneasy. It's the look of someone who knows they've already won, but I won't go down without a fight. The false king surely knows this and wouldn't come alone, but his army is battling Nerazi and Seriq. Through our link, I can feel that both are alive and well. Either the army has left them behind to come here, or....

The Fallacious has created more than one Revenant Swarm.

Recalling Nerazi's theory that the false king was using his army for recon, I come to the sickening realization that The Fallacious must have created more swarms. *How many of my kind have been harvested for his fucked up cause?* A question to ponder another time as I sweep both Roxy and Alexis protectively behind my solid form. If the bastard wants my mate or her friend, he'll have to come through me first.

A shrieking howl fills my ears, and Alexis cries out at the sound. The hundreds of shades that formed the last Revenant Swarm are nothing compared to what spills into the room now. Hundreds of thousands of Vasura, now just husks of their former selves, crowd into the den, solidifying into one, giant, monstrous creature. The unified swarm turns to its leader, who smirks cruelly.

"Kill him," he commands callously, pointing in my direction.

Alexis screams behind me, not in fright but in rage.

"NO!" she bellows, skirting around me as I frantically try to push her back, reaching out with shadow arms to draw her in.

"Stop!" Roxy yells, mimicking my actions to yank Alexis back to safety.

My mate has no idea this is a foe she can't win against.

Unfortunately, she proves to be the perfect distraction, and the Revenant Swarm strikes when I'm least prepared. The blow to the head knocks me sidewise, sending my senses reeling. Before I can regain my focus, the false king's army attacks. Although the Revenant Swarm lacks emotion, I would swear this particular group is comprised of Vasura made of tenacity. They have one goal—*to end me*—and they won't stop until I'm one of them. But when I peek around the room, The Fallacious is gone, meaning he can't harvest my shadow form if I do fall.

He's not the only one missing.

The Revenant Army is just a distraction.

The false king came to steal Alexis.

He thinks he can just take my mate as his own, but the mark I etched into her flesh says otherwise.

TWENTY
Nerazi

Seriq and I race to help Rastorj.

The arid and empty terrain of The Bowels is devoid of any other creature that dwells in this nightmarish land. Normally, I would take this as a good thing as one doesn't want to encounter these beasts, but their absence heralds a bigger monster. When we finally reach Rastorj, the Revenant Swarm is already over him, slowly sucking the emotion from his body. The Vasura is a dim, grayish-purple hue, and I know he doesn't have much longer until he is a husk and will dissolve into nothing.

Seriq and I exchange a quick glance before lengthening our claws and rushing toward the monstrous horde. It feints right, as if predicting my actions. Every move I make, it counterattacks. Chancing a peek at Seriq, I see he's faring better than me. It's almost as if this swarm knows me.... and then I realize *it does*. This has to be the same reconnaissance army that Xhoshad and I fought against before—it explains why it can mirror me and not Seriq.

Which means I need to throw some new punches.

Luckily, my base emotion is mischief; I'm full of all kinds of different tricks. Disappearing into shadowy mist, I reappear over the entity while forming the talons on my left hand into a spear. With deadly precision, I thrust the sharpened tip into the base of the creature's skull where the head meets the neck. I don't decapitate the thing, but cause the head to loll forward as the entity stumbles about before falling to the ground and dispersing into hundreds of screeching shadows. Some escape, while others lie on the blackened ground before dissolving into dust.

Breathing heavily, I check to see if Seriq is alright before crouching down next to Rastorj. His color is still ashy, and I know he must get to his mate and feed if he wants to heal. Communicating silently with Seriq, we each lift one of Rastorj's arms over our shoulders, hoisting him up to walk back to his den. We move as quickly as possible, knowing we are vulnerable like this out in the open. I extend extra shadow limbs to better support Xhoshad's friend, pondering what just happened.

It makes no sense.

The Revenant Swarm attacks under the guise of discipline, but The Fallacious is always not far behind to collect the emotion of the wounded Vasura. The false king uses his army to amass stronger and deadlier base feelings, but was nowhere in sight tonight nor when this same swarm attacked earlier. In fact, it's unheard of for The Fallacious to even be down here. This is the humans' estimation of Hell, and my kind's personal form of imprisonment.

Or it was, before The Fallacious.

Now, instead of banishment, the false king kills you to harvest your emotion. On the one hand, it seems more efficient. On the other hand, it speaks of a greed that even I cannot fathom—*and that's one of my core emotions from which*

I was created. The question circles back as to why The Fallacious has a recon army, and if he has that, does he have more Revenant Swarms with other purposes? The thought twists my stomach, and I turn my head to look at Seriq. His expression says it all.

We fucked up.

The attack on Rastorj was to draw us away from the females. The Fallacious' recon told him there are three of us and one would surely stay behind, but if the false king made more than one army.... We can barely fight a Revenant Swarm with two Vasura. There's no way Xhoshad would have been able to fight and protect Alexis and Roxy if The Fallacious came to him with more than one swarm. Carefully, Seriq and I shift Rastorj so we can become wisps that can fly. Our hold on him is not as secure in this form. Unlike Alexis, who is small and light, Vasura are extremely dense. To carry him in shadow form strains us, and we're more likely to drop the drained man, but there is no question that we must make haste.

When we arrive back at the den, the front door and wall are demolished. Peering inside, I see Xhoshad on his side, unconscious. Gently setting Rastorj down, I rush over to him, dismayed I didn't feel his distress. Even now, I try to taste his pain, but can't get a read on him. I motion for Seriq to come over. He's busy sniffing around the room with manic intent. The Fallacious has never been a fool in my eyes until this moment, but taking our mate was indeed unwise.

"Can you sense Xhoshad?" I ask Seriq when he finally walks over.

All I get in answer is a slash of his head in negation. Reaching out mentally, I try to feel Seriq. His inner rage, so clearly stamped into his features, will be a potent cocktail.

While Vasura do not gain energy from others of our kind, we can still taste the myriad of flavors all our emotions create. Anger is a heady and fiery spice that can't be missed. The flavor is so strong, you can almost smell it before you taste it. With the wrath Seriq is projecting, I should sense it twenty miles apart but I can't, and I'm only twenty steps apart.

"What's happened? Why can't we sense one another anymore?" I bark in mild panic.

Seriq is silent for a moment before he says, "I can't feel Alexis, anymore, either."

His words gut me when I reach out and see that he's right. She's gone—fucking gone—and that bastard who sits on the throne stole her.

"He can't have her," I tremble in fury. "We marked her—*claimed her*—he might be king, but he must still adhere to the rules of Vasuriad. He can't change those. We are governed by the land firstly, intrinsically tied to our realm, and the law states that any female marked by another Vasura has formally staked his claim. A battle for her hand can commence *only* if the female decrees it—and there's no way in hell Alexis would do that. She might not want to be here, but she wants to be with *us*."

Seriq nods in agreement.

"So what do we do?" I demand, still too pissed to think clearly.

"We go to the Palasseum and get our mate back," the green-eyed Vasura responds simply.

I blink at how obvious it is; unfortunately, both Rastorj and Xhoshad are injured and need energy fast, but without any humans, they can't be restored to full health—and going into the lion's den requires one to be in peak performance. The Palasseum is where the false king lives, holds court, and showcases his weekly tournaments where he pits weakened Vasura against creatures from all over Vasuriad. It's also where my kind goes to fight over a mating claim.

But part of me wonders if this isn't just another trap The Fallacious is setting for us.

Xhoshad is still not conscious, but Rastorj's glowing violet eyes stare at me, the light within the large orbs dimming with every passing second. I want to reassure him that everything is ok—that everything will be fine—but I can't find it in myself to give him this kind lie. It's better to brainstorm with Seriq a plan on how to get both Vasura out of The Bowels and across The Malevolands.

Assuming the Revenant Swarm isn't waiting for us at the border.

Growling, I wonder if that's The Fallacious' plan when an eerie howl reverberates around the destroyed room. Soon, there's another, and another, and another, until the very ground vibrates and trembles with the sound.

"What the fuck is that?" I burst out.

"Scurion," Seriq supplies, and my blood runs cold.

Scurion are the most dangerous creatures in The Bowels. Their eight, segmented legs allows them to crouch low to the ground, but they easily tower over fifteen feet high when standing tall. Atop the thorax—where the legs connect—is the head. A cross between a spider and a crocodile in the human world, this eyeless monstrosity hunts via sound and smell. The demonic beast has a taste for Vasura, according to legend, but is rare to spot and is generally a solitary animal.

Yet, here come four, barreling toward Rastorj's damaged dwelling.

The Bowels are large. These creatures couldn't have come here at the same time by hapchance. Something drove them to us. My first guess is The Fallacious, but again, why? If we're attacked and consumed by these ugly, terrible things, the false king will never be able to use our base emotions. Perhaps we are expendable; perhaps he would prefer we die in The Bowels than challenge him at his Palasseum—*either way, this means another fight.*

Without Alexis to replenish our energy, I already feel defeated. Pessimism isn't one of my core emotions, but I'm synching up with the sensation, making me wonder if perhaps this is Rastorj's base for creation and he's projecting it, even wounded. The wounded Vasura sucks in a hissing breath, the wheezing sound whistling through the air. There's a sickly rattle to it, and even if Seriq and I are lucky enough to escape with Xhoshad and him, I doubt Rastorj will make it in time to his mate.

He'll starve to death.

"Get up!" I hear Seriq roar.

The sound startles me—and Xhoshad—enough so that he comes to. My red-eyed friend blinks in confusion before screaming for our mate.

"She's gone—The Fallacious took her," I yell over his bellow. "We'll get her back, but right now, we have bigger problems."

I tip my head toward the scurions who are almost upon us. Xhoshad takes in the situation before dispersing into a smoky silhouette.

"Grab Rastorj," he orders.

"You're too weak—" I counter, but Xhoshad hisses viciously, cutting me short.

"I'm still strong enough from the claiming," he spits, "but I'm not strong enough to fight off four scurions. Let's grab Rastorj and get the fuck out of here!"

Seriq follows suit; sighing, I do the same, hoping we can

get out of this alive. The three of us float over to Rastorj and pick him up. Xhoshad's hold on him wobbles before he can steady himself. I don't know how far we'll get, but Xhoshad will have to rest in The Malevolands. He's right that feasting from Alexis during her claiming has fortified him, but he'll still need time to recover from carrying Rastorj out of here.

The scurions let out frenzied yowls of anger at our escape, but I don't even look back down at them. Swiftly, my trium pushes out of the humid depths of The Bowels into the much cooler Malevolands. Seriq navigates to a odollam tree, and we set Rastorj down once safely absconded beneath the leaves. He's barely breathing and all color has been leached from his normally deep purple skin.

"I…. I can't feel my mate," he rasps weakly. "She's dead."

His conclusion makes Xhoshad jump up in alarm.

"I can't feel Alexis!" he cries in anguish, but I raise a hand to silence him.

"Our bonds have been…. muted," I explain, unsure of the right word to use.

"Muted?' the scarlet-eyed Vasura echoes.

"Yes, try to feel for me or Seriq," I command and see Xhoshad trying.

"I can't sense you at all!" he exclaims.

"The Fallacious must have done something—"

"But what is the question," Seriq finishes.

"Your mate is not dead," I reassure Rastorj. "Don't give up hope. She needs you."

He nods weakly, acknowledging my words.

"What happened?" Xhoshad demands, and I fill him in; then listen to his story, trying to piece the two sides together.

"None of it makes sense," I conclude. "What is The Fallacious up to?"

"I don't know," he murmurs, "but I don't like it. We can

figure it out later. Right now, we need to get Alexis and Roxy back."

"We must fight," Seriq adds, and Xhoshad lowers his head.

"No Vasura has won a mating match at the Palasseum."

"Until now," I grin, my sharp teeth grinding together in menace.

"Until now," Seriq agrees with a lethal smile.

It's time to reclaim our mate once and for all.

TWENTY-ONE
Alexis

"Roxy," I whisper. "Roxy! Can you hear me?"

A soft moaning sound is the only indication that she's nearby.

"It's over, Lexie," she whispers mournfully. "We're doomed."

I blink into the darkness, overwhelmed by her cynical outlook. The Fallacious flew us to his palace—according to Roxy—and locked us in a room. But since I can't see, I have no idea what the place looks like, effectively making it impossible for me to run and escape. I have no idea even the direction I need to go. Unfortunately, Roxy is no help.

"Rox! Snap out of it, we have to get to the guys!"

"There's nothing to return to.... Rastorj is dead," she answers dully.

"How can you know that?" I demand.

"Because I can't feel him."

She doesn't expound upon her words, and I have no clue how to process them.

"How would you "feel" him?" I prompt after a minute.

"Through my mark. You have three from your mates. Now that you've been claimed, your connection should be even stronger. You should be able to sense their erm, essence, I guess."

I close my eyes, tuning into the marks on my body, envisions Xhoshad, Seriq, and Nerazi in my mind, but don't feel a single thing—*except ridiculous.*

"Well, they're all ok," I tell my best friend stoutly, "and they're coming to rescue us."

"They better get here soon. I heard The Fallacious whispering on the way here. He plans to publicly mark and claim you."

I gasp.

"What? What does that *mean*?!"

"You're the lost heir, Lex, if he takes you as his mate, his claim to the throne becomes legitimate. Those who oppose him won't have a leg to stand on."

"Bu-bu-but, I've already been claimed!" I splutter, cringing at the words.

"Unless your mates show up to fight for you, the false king will consider their absence a forfeit for your hand— and you better hope they don't come. The Palasseum is The Fallacious' seriously fucked up castle where he makes Vasura fight one another and unspeakable creatures from the land in a large arena while his loyal subjects watch. It's like Gladiator, but worse."

I wince at her words.

Where the fuck am I?

"Then we'll have to escape ourselves," I decide firmly.

Before Roxy can respond, I hear a door open, and someone slithers into the room. I close my eyes, inhaling deeply and holding my breath. Childishly, I think it can shut the intruder out. A clawed finger brushes lightly down the side of my face, and I know it's *him*.

"I'd like to speak with you in private," The Fallacious hisses to me before addressing Roxy. "I'll return for your friend later."

She sniffles at his words, and my anger returns tenfold. No one likes a bully, and his actions bring me back to my teens years when the helplessness of my situation made me tremble with repressed ire.

"Don't touch her," I command sternly.

The monster king pauses, his bright blue eyes assessing me. Through their light, I can make out the flatness of his nose, his sharp, white teeth, and a jagged mark down the left side of his cheek. It reminds me of the marks Xhoshad, Nerazi, and Seriq put on me, and I wonder if it's a scar or a mating mark. A cruel, amused smile graces his lips.

"I won't touch her—but others might," he sings.

Without thinking, I lunge, my fury getting the best of me. My head reaches only his stomach, but I lower it like a charging bull. I'm intent on ramming into his most sensitive area, but the false king can see where I can't. A shadow limb snakes out to catch and stop me. He chuckles, pissing me off more.

"Come, we must get you dressed," he decrees, sweeping me out of the room and away from Roxy.

I'd forgotten I am once more naked, but don't care. I need to get back to my best friend. She's lost all hope, and I'm afraid of what will happen to her now. The Fallacious takes me down a long hall and a flight of stairs and into another room. Once there, he begins circling me like a hawk.

"I have something for you, but first, allow me to introduce myself. I am King Zuriv, and you, my human beauty, will be my queen. Together, we will rule over all of Vasuriad," he announces, coming over to place a hand on my stomach. "And someday, you will carry the heir to the throne after I plant my seed deep inside your womb."

His words hang between us like a horrible prophesy.

"I highly doubt that's going to happen!" I snap at his archaic thought process.

The only way this monster is impregnating me is against my will—*and I'll fight him tooth and nail before he ever gets a chance.*

"DON'T YOU EVER FUCKING DOUBT ME!" the psycho screams, globs of spittle dripping down the side of his mouth and spewing onto my face.

I cringe, wiping them away with the back of my hand, trying to inch back. Clearly, the false king is not mentally stable—especially if he thinks I'm his queen. The Fallacious takes a moment to regain his composure, his bright eyes trained on me the entire time. His irritation melts away to a more pleasant mask, reminding me of Nerazi, but my yellow-eyed monster merely pretends to be naughty. This thing before me is pure evil pretending to be good.

"Don't doubt me," he repeats in a more genial tone. "Now, *my queen*, I have a gift for you."

He walks to somewhere in the room, but of course, I can't see where or what he's doing, but when he pulls out a glowing vial, I snap to attention.

"Do you know what this is?" he asks, and I shake my head, drinking in the lovely light the vial gives off. "It's a little potion made of sinqol, the organism from our realm that makes it so Vasura can see."

Vaguely, I recall Roxy saying something about the incandescent substance. The Fallacious holds it close to my face, and it illuminates his long, deadly claws. I'm wondering how I can steal the vial and use it to help me see and escape, when something grabs my hair, pulling and yanking my head back. I realize too late it's the false king.

His giant form hovers over my upturned head, his glowing eyes alight with interest—and anything that intrigues this monster curdles my insides. Without warning, he dumps the contents of the vial over my eyes. I scream at the searing pain as The Fallacious releases me, and I sink to my knees in agony.

"It burns!" I whimper, convinced he's blinded me.

The callous bastard just laughs.

"It's supposed to," he calls lightly, making me want to stab him repeatedly with a dull, blunt object.

I have no idea how long I writhe on the floor in pain, but eventually, it subsides. My harsh and labored breathing is the only sound in the room, and I wonder if the false king has left. For his sake, I hope he has. When I finally blink open my eyes, I feel them widen in amazement.

I can see!

The room is ornate, but gloomy. The walls are black, embellished with demonic carvings that seem alive. It appears to be devoid of any furnishings—devoid of anything really—except for the fucker who poured liquid sinqol into my eyes and a single table with a drawer.

And helped me see.

He's standing in the corner, a shoulder propped up against the wall, observing me. His glowing blue eyes don't seem so bright now. Instead of being naked, he's dressed in what looks like a Native American chieftain headdress and robes. The sight reminds me that I'm bare, and I quickly peek down. Gasping, I attempt to shield my breasts and pussy from his hungry eyes. Before, the darkness blinded me into thinking I wasn't exposed, but now I see what my monsters see....

And every other bogeyman.

"No need to hide yourself from me, my queen. What's yours is mine, and what's mine is....still mine. I don't share well, but you'll learn. Now, one more thing before the tournaments."

My mind scrambles to keep up with his cryptic and disturbing words. The Fallacious goes back to the table and pulls out yet another vial. Instinctively, I shy away. To be fair, the last thing he took from there helped me, but I don't trust this monstrous man at all. He walks over, holding the unknown fluid aloft.

"No need to fear this. I've put it on you before."

This brings me up short.

"Um, when?"

"Oh, I forgot you were unconscious," he smirks, and my blood congeals.

When was I ever unconscious in his presence?!

I don't remember a time I wasn't alert—the jerk has to be lying. Warily, I scope out the door, calculating my escape, when he darts into my personal space faster than lightning. I only have time to gasp before he's rubbing *something* into my neck over Seriq's mark. It tingles, but there's no pain. Before I can react, he does the same to Xhoshad's mark on my stomach and then spins me around to touch Nerazi's.

"What are you doing?" I demand in outrage at his nerve.

"Numbing your bond," he replies without remorse.

I process his words, recalling Roxy's, and a lightbulb goes off in my head.

"This is why Rox can't feel Rastorj!"

"Mmmm, clever girl," the king purrs.

"They'll come for us," I spit at him in outrage, but he grins.

"Good, that's what I want. Their despair grows, enhancing their core emotion, until they are blinded by their own hate. It'll eat them alive; then, they'll be ready to fight—*for me.*"

"You sound.... incredibly unstable," I confess, "and I have no clue what you're talking about."

"I'm building an unstoppable army," he supplies.

"The, um, Revenant Swarm?"

"Yes and no."

His answer makes me scowl.

"I don't know what you're planning, but my monsters won't fall for it—and I'll *never* be your queen."

"Never say never," he tuts, and I repress the urge to throat punch him—mostly because I can't reach and will likely only hurt myself. "You'll be my queen because you'll have no choice."

"Do you really think by making me your mate that you'll become a true king?!" I demand.

The Fallacious cocks his head, assessing me.

"What do you mean by that, human?"

His soft voice sends chills down my spine.

"I, uh, know why they call you The Fallacious."

"Do you," he hums, and I wonder if perhaps I know nothing at all. "They don't call me this because I'm not the true king, but because I was born of deception and lies. I assure you no one is better fit to sit on the Vasuriad throne than me."

"So you're the lost heir?" I snark.

"My, my, you are informed. No, I'm not the lost heir—as the title suggests, the heir is gone and will never return.

Therefore, the throne goes to the next in line—which happens to be *me*."

Sucking in my lower lip, I ponder his words.

"How.... so?" I inquire.

"Because—my brother was king. Without a child to succeed him, it naturally defaults to me. My brother tried to destroy this world and our food source. By mating to human women, Vasura don't need to visit the human realm for sustenance anymore—but we need the humans. They are a banquet of delicious emotions for us to feast upon. A mindless horde of unaware sheep that I will someday control—and that, my queen, is my why I'm king. I will take Vasuriad to the next level and conquer the human realm, enslaving those who created us."

I clasp my hands behind my back to hide their tremble. The Fallacious is unhinged—and holds absolute power—the single worst combination ever.

"But I still don't understand why you need me then...."

"Every king needs a queen, right? And an heir. I need a successor for my throne—someone that nobody will contend when he ascends to it someday. Someone who will maintain my vision. Someone I can trust."

I swallow thickly at his words.

"Is this because of who I am really?"

The Fallacious stills at my words.

"Who told you?" he hisses, poofing into smoke and reappearing inches from my face.

Startled, I jerk away, tripping into the wall. It yawns and moans, making me scream. I look at the embellished carvings to see them wriggling and twisting about.

"What the fuck?!" I scream.

The king comes up to draw me back.

"Careful, these are just some of the Vasura that I've trapped, waiting to use for my army."

Staring in horror, I look around the room, realize the walls are made up entirely of the silhouetted forms of bogeymen. Zuriv grabs my shoulder and spins me around.

"Who told you?" he repeats.

"Roxy," I confess, and the king looks thoughtful at my words.

"Her mate must have told her.... and your mates must have told him—meaning they will covet you even more. No matter, though," he dismisses. "I'm ready to fight. That is, if your Vasura even ever make it. We'll see. In the meantime, you'll stay in this room. Don't go near the walls or the door. I'd hate for your soul to be eaten before I have a chance to taste it."

With this, he sweeps out of the room, leaving me frightened and perturbed.

Roxy was right.

I am the lost heir.

TWENTY-TWO
Seriq

"I don't like the plan."

Ignoring Nerazi, I lean over Rastorj, checking his vitals. The Vasura doesn't have much longer—we must get his mate.

"I said, I don't li—"

"We heard you," I snap in irritation.

Nerazi narrows his yellow eyes in menace at me, but shuts up.

"We all have a part," Xhoshad huffs. "Besides, staying here with Rastorj will endear you to his mate—"

"I don't want to be endeared to *her*," Nerazi mutters, but Xhoshad continues like he didn't say anything at all.

"And *that* will endear you to *our* mate," he concludes.

Nerazi ponders this, a frown marring his forehead. I understand his reticence because there's no fucking way I would stay behind, but he's not strong enough to fight me or smart enough to counter Xhoshad's logic. The crimson-eyed Vasura is the unspoken leader of our trium. The false king will be expecting him—*and the rest of us*—which is why only he can go. Xhoshad once was a part of the old king's court. He knows the ins and outs of the politics and other unscrupulous activities held at the Palasseum.

To The Fallacious, it will seem only he chose to come and fight, but in reality, I will follow. My kind can become one with the shadows, but I am the very darkness that humans fear. If I will it, no one will see me. Xhoshad is the diversion, and I'm the predator from the night. Nerazi isn't stealthy enough to pull off this mission, nor well-known enough to present himself to the false king, and so he must stay behind and be pissy about it. Still, I understand his ire —Alexis is his mate, too—but we risk too much going in all together. The truth is, if Xhoshad or I are captured, we're counting on Nerazi to save our asses.

This is where his mischievous streak comes in handy.

I've seen the destruction and the havoc he's wreaked, so much so you would think he was born of chaos. As the youngest in our trium, Xhoshad and I tend to underestimate his abilities. Nerazi was born eons ago after human civilizations were formed and settled—there must be stability before humans default into troublemaking. It's inherent to their self-destructive nature. They ban together to create kingdoms, and then slowly pick it apart until it crumbles.

Nerazi was born from these obstreperous shambles.

Xhoshad was created long before this stability among humans was reached. He was born from the underhanded fighting tactics humans used to gain power. Coercion is not as deadly as some of the other core emotions a Vasura can be formed from—but it's just as powerful—especially if one knows how to wield it effectively, and Xhoshad is a master of his trade. He can see into your soul and know exactly how to manipulate you. He is a human's concept of a siren enchanting you with his words.

You are compelled to do as he commands, and by the time you realize your mistake—it's too late.

Then, there's me, the oldest of us all, born from the earliest of human emotions. Since the dawn of time, human man has looked for something to claim as his own. *Is it any wonder why my kind is covetous—why I'm so avarice?* We've learned from the masters. Humans have destroyed worlds to possess more. Before Alexis, I operated solely on the emotion ingrained into my psyche, but now I understand human behavior on another level.

She is mine, and I will slaughter all who stand in my way to get to my mate—starting with the false king.

"Let's go," I command Xhoshad.

I grow impatient to hold Alexis in my arms once more, as do the others. With one last look at Rastorj and Nerazi, I shift into nothing but a silhouette and soar into the sky with Xhoshad. Together, we race to the Palasseum, knowing that time is of the essence. When we near the towering castle made of enslaved Vasura, I feel my hand solidify and my talons lengthen. I will myself to remain calm. Although my kind is monstrous, we were never truly monsters until The Fallacious.

He is turning us into ruthless savages, little better than the humans.

"It's time," Xhoshad whispers before flying ahead.

Plummeting to the ground, I flatten myself into the darkness there, merging with the slight shadows that exist in our world. It takes forever to cross into the courtyard and inside the palace, but eventually I make my way to the throne room where The Fallacious sits, Xhoshad kneeling before him.

"I've come to take my mate—the one you stole from me!"

The false king laughs as if amused, but I can taste his annoyance.

Was this not what he wanted?

"She's not your mate," he counters lightly, making Xhoshad roar in anger.

"My mark on her stomach says otherwise!" he snarls.

Vasura claws are like human fingerprints—unique to each of us—therefore, mating marks are unique to the one who made it on his woman. For The Fallacious to contend this is unspeakable—*a slap to the face.*

"I didn't see any mark," the false one taunts, and I see Xhoshad clench his hand into fists.

Blood drips from his curled palms where his talons pierced his purple flesh.

"Don't bait me, Zuriv," he spits, refusing to use The Fallacious' title. "My mate doesn't have just one mark, but three, and no Vasura could've missed them. Bring her here."

The bastard grins coldly.

"Of course. Let me go retrieve her. In the meantime, would you like a snack?" He motions to a servant, who scurries away to bring in Rastorj's mate. Her skin is deathly pale and her eyes are wide and sightless. "The Barren One is useless as anything but food, but I just remembered you're challenging me. I don't want you to be any stronger, so no snacking for you. Take her away."

The Fallacious cackles maniacally as he departs. Xhoshad discreetly looks in my direction. Although our bond is damaged for some reason, he still knows my methods and mannerisms. Quietly, I slip from the room and follow the false king. First, he stops to ensure Rastorj's mate is secured, not that she's in any condition to escape—he merely wants to taunt her more.

"Your friend tells me that you know who she is—to the

Vasura, to *me*," he growls, circling her. "How did you find out?"

Roxy doesn't respond, perhaps too weak to do so.

"Did your mate tell you?"

"No," she finally croaks. "I guessed.... from the stories he told."

The Fallacious stops pacing, as if intrigued by her words. "Stories? What stories?"

"Of the lost heir."

I suck in a breath, nearly blowing my cover.

Alexis is.... *the lost heir?*

Zuriv smiles in delight.

"I see. How very *clever* of you," he commemorates Roxy. "If you'll excuse me."

He exits the room, and I scramble to keep up, my mind reeling. If Alexis is truly the lost heir, then The Fallacious is her uncle—*and he wants to claim her as his mate*. My mouth forms a grim line at the horror of it all. I follow him until he enters another room where Alexis is sitting in the middle, staring at nothing in particular. Her eyes are glowing, brighter than even her friend's who's been here for over ten years, and I feel ill looking at her.

What did this bastard do to my mate?

"Alexis, there's someone here to see you," he croons.

Her head snaps up.

"I told you they would come," she says without a hint of fear that makes me smile.

"Well, only one of them came," Zuriv tuts.

"So you think," she mumbles incoherently under her breath.

The Fallacious doesn't hear her, but I do, and I want nothing more than to take her into my arms and kiss her senseless. My brave, wise mate is staying strong and trusting us—more than I could ever ask for. The Fallacious has his back to her, pulling out a small bottle of something before turning back to her.

"And so, we must battle for your hand," he continues. "If Xhoshad wins, you're free to go with him. If not.... *you're mine.*"

He says this last part as he smears whatever is in the vial over the mark—*my mating mark*—on Alexis' neck. I realize it's barely visible, slowly vanishing before my sight. This coupled with his last words blinds me to the plan—blinds me to everything but one thing.

Reclaiming my mate.

I spring from the shadows, solidifying with a roar that thunders around the room, startling my mate.

But not The Fallacious.

"SHE IS MINE!" I howl.

The bastard smirks in a way that says I've just played right into his hand. He was expecting this, and I curse myself a fool.

"Seriq! So good of you to join us. I was just getting Alexis here so we could begin the fight. Swarm—take him to the arena!"

Before I can react, the walls come alive, the trapped Vasura flying from them to form a giant entity who picks me up, trapping me. The false king sweeps up my mate, cradling her in his arms before marching out of the room, his Revenant Swarm following. I am ceremoniously escorted to the Palasseum's arena where Xhoshad is already waiting, chained to a pillar. I struggle against the entity's hold, but it's futile. Soon, I'm bound just like my red-eyed friend. I bellow so loudly that the stands full of watching Vasura quakes beneath my rage. The Fallacious reappears above me in a special seating area, my mate at his side.

"THAT'S MY MATE! SHE IS MINE!" I repeat.

The bastard king stands, holding up his arms for silence before replying.

"I don't see any mating marks on her," he smirks.

Next to me, Xhoshad sucks in a ragged breath, piecing together what has happened.

"She is my mate—mark or no mark—and I will prove it. Zuriv the Deceitful, I challenge *you* for Alexis the Human Female!"

The Vasura watching stare at the king, waiting to see what he does, but he merely waves a dismissive hand.

"So be it," he decrees, preparing to sit down, but I stop him.

"No! I challenged you—*not your army*. Are you too weak and scared to fight me yourself?"

The Fallacious narrows his glowing blue eyes at me. He played into the weakness of my base emotion, but I just played into *his*—*vanity can be a bitch*. After a moment, he bows his head toward me.

"Very well, Seriq the Possessive. You will regret this decision, I'm sure."

He pulls Alexis into the shadows, and I strain to see my mate. The Fallacious disappears, and I grow uneasy. Minutes later, the false king reappears on the far edge of the arena and walks toward me. He waves a hand at the Revenant Swarm who unchains me. The second my hands are free I rush at the despicable bastard. I form my claws into long knives, intent on carving my mark into him—the punishment for erasing the one on my mate—but he easily sidesteps me, as if predicting my move. This happens over and over until I'm so blinded with raw fury, I can barely see anymore.

How does he know what I'm going to do?

Changing tactics, I reach out with my shadow limbs and become one with the darkness inside of me. I lash out, restraining his arms and legs. He struggles, and I wait for him to dissolve into a smoky wisp, but he surprises me by staying solid. I attack quickly, using my talons to sever through the flesh and bone at his neck. The Fallacious stumbles, his head lolling, before falling forward and rolling in the sand. The crowd gasps as I tip my head back and roar in victory. I look at Xhoshad, drunk with power, when I see his expression. Turning around, I watch Zuriv's body vanish before my eyes.

Just like my mark on Alexis' throat.

A taunting, echoing laugh fills the arena, and I realize this wasn't the real king. All this time we crowned him the deceitful one—The Fallacious—but in reality, his core emotion is illusion—*lies through deception*. Without thinking, I launch myself into the stands where Alexis still sits in the shadows, but the instant I touch her, she too vanishes. Incensed at my own stupidity, I shred the blood-red curtains that hang around me decoratively.

I destroy everything in sight, not stopping until I look back in the arena to see Xhoshad is gone. I freeze, knowing he didn't leave of his own accord. My mate and brother were stolen right from under my nose, and I have no way of tracking them. I sink to my knees in defeat, debating what to do, before dissolving into shadows and wisping away. I fly back to Nerazi and Rastorj.

"Where's Alexis?" the yellow-eyed Vasura demands, but I say nothing.

The answer is obvious.

Quietly, I sit down next to Rastorj. I let him down, too. I sink into a silent depression, for underneath my core emotion of possessiveness lies another.

Worthlessness.

And never have I felt so useless in my existence as I do in this moment.

Nerazi walks over, crouching at my side.

"What happened?"

Haltingly, I tell him in as few words as possible, not wanting to put words to the memories that will forever haunt me. Nerazi doesn't say anything when I'm done, and I can taste his disappointment—*because I failed*. We sit there, watching Rastorj slowly die, and I wish it were me. Eventually, Nerazi gets up, walking over the low-hanging odollam branch. Eyeing them speculatively, he turns back to me.

"Alexis isn't the lost heir," he finally announces.

Startled from my misery, I ask how he knows this. The mischievous Vasura grins.

"Because Rastorj used to live at The Palasseum, long before the lost heir. He says there were rumors of a female called The Pharos—a beacon to heal our realm and make us no longer dependent on humans."

"A myth," I interject.

"That's what I thought, too, but—"

"What?"

"She bears the mark," Rastorj croaks, surprising me.

I look quizzically at Nerazi.

"Rastorj saw a symbol depicting The Pharos and drew it as a sign of hope when he and Roxy lived in The Bowels—a symbol Roxy attests Alexis has at the nape of neck, under her hair."

"Roxy told The Fallacious that Alexis is the lost heir," I counter, and Rastorj rouses more.

"My mate is alive?"

I blanch.

"Yes," I reply simply.

What more can I say without destroying his hopes?

"She misunderstood," Rastorj coughs. "Alexis is the beacon; we can't let the false king use her."

I shake my head, confused.

"What will he do with Alexis?"

Rastorj stares at me with glowing purple eyes full of despair and premonition.

"Destroy our world—*through her.*"

Wordlessly, Nerazi and I stand.

"We have to find our mate," he says flatly. "This time, *you* stay with Rastorj."

I nod—*I deserve nothing less.*

Nerazi shifts into shadow form, flitting out of the odollam tree and into the surrounding darkness while I hunker down with the dying Vasura. I've always yearned for silence, but now wish I had someone to fill it with chatter. My thoughts are too loud, too self-deprecating. I must fix this, but I don't know how. Rastorj thankfully interrupts my painful, internal worries.

"Get me to a portal," Rastorj requests.

I hesitate.

"Most are not working, and it's hard to find humans who believe in us anymore. You can sense their emotions, but aren't able to feed from them. It is.... agony," I finish, but Rastorj waves a weak hand.

"I have a plan," he counters.

Debating what to do, I eventually scoop him into my arms before dissolving into smoke. There is one portal very rarely monitored back near the Palasseum. Perhaps because of its location The Fallacious assumes no one will be foolish enough to use it. Then again, the false king has proven himself to be smarter than he looks. I won't make the mistake of underestimating him again. When we reach the portal, I sit in the shadows with Rastorj, scanning the area. I'm about to ask him what his plan is when the portal yawns open. Staring in shock, I watch as a human male steps through—the first to enter our realm. Even from a distance, I can taste his emotions and instantly know who it is.

Alexis' old boyfriend.

Beside me, Rastorj groans.

"Ah, fuck, what terrible timing."

I blink, confused.

"Do you know who that is?"

Rastorj nods.

"The lost heir."

My mind blanks.

Things just got a thousand times more complicated.

CHAPTER TWENTY-THREE
Mark

"Here's my two weeks' notice."

I politely set down my resignation in front of the head of the board of directors before pivoting on my heel to walk away. I'm in a rush, but the man isn't letting me off that easily.

"Dr. Bradley—please reconsider! This hospital will be lost without you. We need you—I need you. You're slated to take my position at the end of the year," he reminds. "Think of all you've worked for."

Hanging my head, I slowly turn to address him.

"I.... know, but my heart isn't in it anymore. Do you really want an ER surgeon who doesn't have his head in the game?" I joke.

"Your father will be so disappointed," the man points out.

A wry smile twists my lips at his words.

"My father has made his thoughts abundantly clear. I believe I've gone above and beyond to make him proud—"

"I apologize, Mark," the director interjects. "I didn't

mean to say your dad isn't pleased with your success, but the two of you worked side-by-side to restore this hospital to its former glory. When your dad retired, he handed me the keys, but you the reins. You're the one who runs the show—I just lock up at night."

"All of this has weighed heavily on me, but I've made my decision. I've already found a replacement, an excellent doctor fresh from grad school with stellar grades—all he needs is the experience, but he'll learn quickly. That's the thing about ER doctors. It's a sink or swim job, and within twenty minutes, you're usually paddling along. By the time twenty hours passes, you're a pro. There's never a lack of practice, sadly."

"Would you consider making this only an interim?" the director pleads, but I shake my head.

I won't budge on this because I don't want to lie. I'm leaving—and I know wherever I'm going, I'm never coming back. Either I'm saving Alexis or I'm going to die trying, but she isn't *here* anymore. Not in Texas, not in the US, and maybe not even in this same universe. Quantum physics is a tricky bitch, but once you can grasp the basics, you realize the world how we view it is not how it is in reality. Our world is layered with many others. It's not out of the realm of possibility that Lexie was taken to another dimension. The problem is finding her and getting there.

Luckily for me, I know a man who, ironically, is named Doc Brown.

"Sorry, Paul. It's nothing personal, but I know I'm not coming back."

The director sighs.

"I spoke with Deputy Briggs, son, there are no leads. *None.* Alexis Stanton is gone."

Don't I know this better than anyone.

"Thank you for your time. I know you're a busy man. If you'll please excuse me."

Turning to leave once more, the director stands, coming around to clap a hand on my shoulder.

"Mark, you can't go. This will kill your parents, and after all they did to get you—all they sacrificed to give you."

The guilt is a familiar feeling, lingering in the background against the backdrop of all my tempest of current emotions. I ponder Paul's words. A close friend and associate of my father, I'm sure he already knew days in advance that I planned to quit. He also speaks the truth about my parents. I'm their only child, adopted when I was just an infant. My childhood was spent idyllically basking in their love. My father was a doctor and raised me with the hope I would follow his footsteps. Of course, I did so, partly out of obligation and partly because I enjoyed helping others.

I'm good at my job, one of the best in the state, but no matter what I do, this place doesn't feel like home. Nowhere does. The only time I've felt one hundred percent at peace in my world is when I was with Alexis. There is no rhyme or reason, but she's always been the air that I breathed. When she moved away, I fell apart. At first, I convinced myself that she would return. When she didn't, I set out to prove myself to her. I became the best surgeon, lauded with the steadiest hands in the United States two years in a row, but my accolades never reached her in Australia.

It took her dad getting sick and me begging him to call Alexis to bring her back to the States. Even then, it was the front desk nurse—urged by me—that ended up making contact. I knew if I reached out, she wouldn't come. Now, knowing what she was fleeing, I'm surprised Lexie even stepped foot back on Texan soil. She's a braver soul than me.

Perhaps it's that singular beauty of it that calls to me. I need Alexis like I need oxygen. I can't tell my parents, who've raised me selflessly since birth, that I don't feel like a family.

I love my mom and dad, but I love Alexis more.

The first time I met Lexie was when we were in kindergarten. Another boy was picking on me, taking my toy. I was too much of a pushover to say anything, but not Alexis. She marched right over and demanded the kid give me back my stuff. She stole my heart with her big blue eyes and long, wavy blond hair. Lexie was quiet and sweet, but always self-assured. As we grew older, we became friends. Both of us had similar interests and excelled at school.

In high school, I tried to get closer, but was forever awkward. Luckily, there was Roxy to bridge the gap. She was the daughter of a good family friend of my parents, so we grew up together. She and Lexie were glued to the hip at school. My freshman year was me just trying to get my foot in the door—I just wanted Alexis to see me as something more than a friend. Then, our sophomore year, her mom got sick. Of course, I knew. My dad was the chief of the hospital. Whispers flew about her illness, but Alexis seemed oblivious.

Looking back on it, this was the time she pulled into herself. Roxy and I assumed it was because she knew about her mom—although she never said anything and we never spoke about it—but now I wonder if it wasn't that at all. *How long had these monsters been tormenting Alexis?* When I finally found the gumption to ask her out our senior year, I was over the moon when she agreed. Although occasionally reserved, she never exhibited anything that would alert me that something truly was amiss in her world.

Like monsters living under her bed.

When she first told me who—or what—took Roxy, I

didn't believe her, but Alexis isn't a liar. Nor do I think she's crazy or overcome with grief. She wholeheartedly believes something took Roxy, but when Lexie mysteriously disappeared from her room, I knew she spoke the truth. I searched that house high and low. Alexis Stanton was gone, and monsters took her. After a few shots of Jack, I finally found the courage to call a colleague who works in experimental physics.

Tossing the idea of alternate realms and shadow beings living in them, Kevin boggled my mind not only with the infinite possibilities, but that some scientists have found portals of light that purportedly lead to these other dimensions. Apparently, they've begun experimenting with them to see where they go and if *anything* responds. Nothing so far, but Kevin said there is one portal of particular interest because, unlike the others, it's not made of light, but shadows. It seems to writhe, as if alive, and I know that's my ticket. That small black hole cuts between time and space to take me to Alexis. Kevin thinks I'm nuts, but I know something he doesn't know.

Monsters are real, and they're taking human women.

I've volunteered to be Kevin's human guinea pig. If he can get me through that portal somehow, I promised to tell him what's on the other side—that is, if I can even get back. I'm navigating uncharted waters, but something inside of me tells me this is the direction to go. It's instinctual, and I can't operate on just my brains alone. My human logic must be suspended if I have any hope of finding and rescuing Alexis.

"I'll be back," I promise to Paul.

Although my plans are experimental and borderline crazy, they have to work. I have to find Alexis and save her. Even now, only days later, I have no idea how much time she's spent with these monsters. Time is a fickle concept, shifting and changing more easily than humans perceive. Days here might mean years wherever she is—*years of being subjected to monstrous beasts and their cravings.*

Resentment bubbles inside of me at the thought. Alexis isn't theirs—she's mine. She gave her body to me first, but it's her heart I want, too. *Did she give that to them?* I frown as I leave the director's office, pulling off my tie that feels like it's strangling me at the thought. *Could she really love monsters? If so....*

Could I compete with that?

All that time I thought she and I had something special, when in reality, she was spending her nights with three monstrous men—talking to them, confiding in them, building a relationship with them. Biting the inside of my cheek I remind myself that they stole Roxy and Alexis ran from them for twelve years. She didn't want anything to do with those monsters. I think about our night together, a fire forming in my loins at the mental image of her spread before me.

So much soft flesh to touch.

Those fucking creatures better not be doing that right now. I see red at the thought. Like a bunch of creepers, they stalked her in the dead of night, playing her vulnerabilities against her, but I've known Alexis my whole life—and loved her even longer. I've been her true friend and lover and always will be. When she fled, I gave her space, but I'm done waiting. I know she has feelings for me; they're just buried underneath the trauma of her past. Together, we will piece back her life right after I get her back. Lexie might fear the Bogeymen, but I don't.

I'm going to hunt them down and make them rue the day they ever laid eyes on my girl.

MONSTERS IN MY BED

Book 2 in the Bogeymen series.

CRAVING MORE MONSTERS

CHECK OUT THESE MONSTROUS TITLES

Captured By The Monsters by M.J. Marstens & R.L. Caulder

Soothing Nightmares by M Sinclair

Monsters Within by R.L. Caulder

Friends With The Monsters by Albany Walker

Stolen By Monsters by Eve L. Hart

Run And Hide by Beatrix Hollow

A Lady of Rooksgrave Manor by Katheryn Moon

Monstrum Academy: Year One by A.J. Macey & M.J. Marstens

CRAVING MORE MONSTERS

ABOUT M.J. MARSTENS

USA Today bestselling author M.J. Marstens mixes romance, suspense, comedy, and sassy characters who can say whatever they are thinking because it is just a story. When she is not creating steamy scenes or laugh-out-loud fiascos, she is refereeing her four children that she homeschools. In her free time, she loves to eat, sleep, and pray that her children do not turn out like the characters she writes about in her books. To read more about M.J., please visit these websites and sign-up below!

FACEBOOK
NEWSLETTER
M.J. BOOK LIST

FINAL ACKNOWLEDGEMENTS

I have so many people to thank for this. I want to start with my cover designer who took my idea and made it into something amazingly gorgeous. Thank you.

Thank you to my Smutketeers for leading me down a monstrous path. There is no turning back. Monsters today, butt stuff before noon tomorrow.

The biggest shout out to my alpha and betas. You ladies are my rocks, my sounding board, my everything. Thank you for helping me mold this into an amazing story.

A huge thank you to Mona Brown and H. Fuzhu for creating the art for my book. I love it; it's perfect. I also appreciate the fact someone helped bring my monster porn to life because it was awkward a.f. to ask a stranger to draw some jizzy monster dicks. For them, probably. Not for me because I am suspended from the reality of social norms, haha.

Thank you to my editors and formatter for putting the finishing touches on this book.
And lastly, thank you to you for reading!
xoxo

Some parting monster cock by H. Fuzhu of Seriq and Lexie

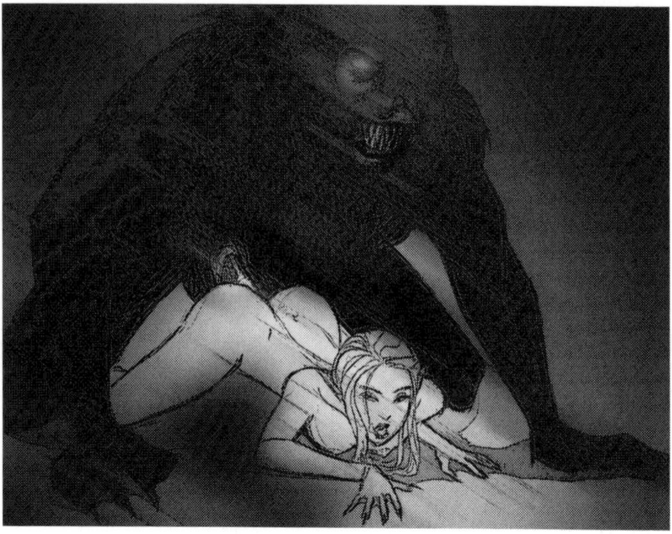

Printed in Great Britain
by Amazon